Mortal Dire

Book Two : Delgado

Cory C. Kovacs

Cover by, Tommy Davis

This is the second book in the Mortal Dire series and also in my writing career. It is dedicated to anyone who has ever had a dream and dared to follow it. To anyone who has loved and lost, and dared to love again. To anyone who has, against all odds, succeeded in doing what others said was impossible. To anyone who has tried, failed, and tried again. And lastly, to anyone who has fought their own demons and beaten them. Don't ever give up, and always have faith. Sometimes it's all we have left.

Failure is not being "unsuccessful"... Failure is when you "stop trying".. ~ C.K.

Everyone has demons and darkness in their lives... It is part of us. We must face them, embrace them, understand them, respect them, be humble to them, learn from them... If we do not, they will haunt us forever and cause us to make poor choices in our futures, hold us back, and destroy us. There can be no light, without the darkness.. ~ C.K. '15.

Contents

Introduction

"**D**elgado", is the second book in the Mortal Dire series. The story brings John and Zed back to the small town of Dyer. Since their last visit, John and Zed find the vacant village is now flourishing. With new businesses, construction, and the new "Greater Dyer Church of God" led by Preacher Bob.

During the demolition of the old Dyer church, a small locked chest was discovered. Preacher Bob does his best to get the message to John, knowing Zed had found the possible key. However, someone else finds this out as well. A vengeful and powerful evil invades Dyer to claim what is in the chest.

As John prepares to wage a battle once again to save the town, he must also contend with his own demons. Unexpectedly, a struggle ensues with his greatest enemy, himself.

Is John's faith in himself and his companions strong enough to overcome the sinister abomination and discover the mysterious contents of the chest before it's too late? Only God knows.

Cory Kovacs presents, Mortal Dire, book two, "Delgado."

Preface

After writing my first "Mortal Dire" book, I was unsure. But a short time after, my confidence began to build. With steady sales and above average reviews, I regreted not becoming a published writer sooner.

The stories that I have and want to tell (and write), are endless. And at times, it takes everything I have not to stop in the middle of a story I am writing, and start on another.

I have definitely learned and keep learning from book one, "Barlos." Most importantly, I have learned discipline. And after completion of book two, "Delgado," I see the "rough" edges of its predecessor. But that's part of the magic. A stepping stone to hopefully becoming a Master of the craft.

This sets the stage for book two. A more "polished" and deeper, yet darker story that grows from page to page. We see the characters evolve and their relationships become stronger, as they are also tested along the way.

I challenged myself to top book one, and I believe I have done this, although I am still proud of "Barlos."

With this, I hope you will enjoy the "second act" of Mortal Dire, "Delgado." ~ Cory Kovacs

Silent Night

Chapter One

A light snow was falling. It was early evening, in the small village of Creek Wood. The random Christmas lights twinkled on the water's surface of the river that flowed at the base of the small town. Peaceful and quiet it was- though only for a moment...

A holiday party was taking place at the local Legion. The small parking lot was full of vehicles slightly covered with a dusting of fresh, light snow. A black jeep made a slow, sharp turn from the main road into the lot and casually rolled into an unoccupied parking space.

Inside the festively decorated building, an adult-only get to-gether- made up mostly of the townspeople- was getting under-way. People mingled and collected drinks from the open bar as Christmas tunes played through the DJ's elaborate sound sys-tem.

People began to whisper as something was amiss. Eight stran-gers meandered quietly through the crowd to different areas of the building. No one knew who they were, but they were no-ticed and very out of place to the village locals.

Two women, and six men, in their younger years and dressed strangely for the current times, almost seemed to place them-selves equally throughout the crowd strategically. The stran-gers all stood patiently as if waiting for something.

One of the men took his place in front of the exit door to the building. He then stood quietly, looking to the other strangers with a slight smile on his face.

The DJ began to spin Burl Ives's, "Holly Jolly Christmas." As the music started to play, the lights from the DJ's display dimmed and set the room in a festive red and green hue.

As the volume of the music increased, everyone's sense of sight and sound became disorientated enough not to realize what was beginning to happen around them.

Each of the strangers placed themselves discreetly next to a patron of their choice. Looking to the man who stood at the exit door, they each waited for his signal.

With a stern stare, the man grinned slightly and gave his head a settle nod. With this, the group simultaneously bared their fangs and bit into the exposed flesh of their intended victims.

Warm blood sprayed in all directions as the loud festive music muffled slight moans and screams of the crowd. People continued to mingle, drink, and converse as the music and lights provided an excellent cover for the attacking creatures.

Within a few moments, the attacks focused upon another group of unsuspecting patrons. People began to drop to the floor, collapse against the walls, and fall into chairs from shock, or sudden lack of blood as the relentless attacks continued.

A feeding frenzy began to break loose as the strangers became less discrete from the taste of fresh, warm blood. The strangers became increasingly vicious and ravenous as people started to realize the horror that was happening around them.

Screams of terror filled the room, and people began to flee in all directions. Blood sprayed everywhere, and panic filled the air as people realized their escape from the unfolding nightmare was cut off.

People tried to run for the exit, only to be met by the vampire who guarded the door. They were quickly and viciously attacked as they tried to flee the building. After four people became severely mutilated, a small crowd of people corralled themselves into a group. Hastily, they ran down the short hall and into one of the restrooms, barricading the door behind them.

The music skipped and scratched as the DJ's blood-soaked, limp body fell forward onto the turntable and smashed to the floor. A vampire stood behind him with blood-dripping fangs as the festive thumping music stopped.

The eight vampires stood smiling and laughing at the carnage and blood that filled the room. There were random moans of agony and whispers of help from those who were still alive.

Screams of terror could be heard coming from behind the restroom door. "Êtez shooting ifish êful a barrel." (Translated; "Like shooting fish in a barrel.") The lead vampire growled with a smile and motioned for the others to move to the restroom door to finish them all.

As the eight began to move toward the short hall, there was a tinkling of a small Christmas bell that hung from the entrance door. A crisp winter breeze whisked in behind a tall, dark figure that entered into the building.

The vampires stopped and watched as a man dressed in a long black coat walked calmly into the dim light of the room. He wore dark shades and tapped along the floor with a cane. The man walked a few paces forward and stopped next to the decorated pool table.

"Vedo got sêtet fucking kidding êm!" (Translated; "You've got to be fucking kidding me!") One of the vampires mumbled as the others chuckled.

They all looked at each other, smiling and laughing, as the blind man stood silent in the middle of the gruesome scene of bodies and blood.

"Am I too late for the party?" the man asked, breaking the silence. A vampire moved silently toward the man as the others stood to watch the show. "Oh no, you're just in time. The party's just starting." Sinister laughs came from the group. Another vampire moved in to stand next to the man. "But you're not quite dressed for the occasion," one of the vampires said as he retrieved a top hat that fell from a snowman display, gently placing it on the man's head. A moment later, like the wind, the other vampire snatched the man's cane from under his grasp. All of the other creatures began to laugh at the man's embarrassment.

The man was calm as the two vampires stood on either side of him and quietly mocked him. One of the creatures waved his clawed palm in front of the man's face, and there was no response. The other vampire leaned in just inches from the man's bare neck and stuck out his long tongue and bared his fangs to taunt the blind man. "Alês sêtetnêo too easy." (Translated; "This is too easy.") The other vampires all laughed wickedly.

"Are vedo sure den êtes?" (Translated; "Are you sure about that?") The man said calmly as his head turned to face the shocked creature. The vampire's face fell as the other stopped laughing at the man's remark.

With the vampire caught off-guard, the man suddenly pivoted his footing and produced a silver blade in his grasp from his sleeve and thrust upward under the creature's chin. It was an immediate death blow to the vampire as the creature combusted into a burning carcass of unnatural blue and purple flames. The fiend dropped to the floor into a pile of smoldering ash within seconds.

Shock fell upon the group of vampires. The man immediately turned to the pool table, retrieving a pool cue. Using it like a bat, the man swung at the other creature closest to him. The vampire raised his forearm to the man's swing. With a solid hit, the pool cue splintered in half over the creature's solid arm with little effect. The vampire smiled, flashing his fangs to the man. "Now whatcha gonna do, bitch!" With a smile of his own, the man replied, "Watch this!" Shifting his stance and twirling the cue, the man slammed the splintered rod directly into the creature's chest. A look of disgust fell over the vampire's twisted face as he fell to his knees grasping at the splintered cue. Once again, flames engulfed the creature, and within moments, reduced to a pile of hot embers.

Another creature moved in to attack, but the man was ready. With a "click" of his boot heel, a silver stiletto blade protruded from the boot's toe. The man pumped back on his foot and side-kicked directly into the advancing vampire's chest. Again, the creature fell back into a burning heap and then was gone.

The remaining creatures growled and hissed and began to re-group. They began to curse in Vampiric tongue, and their thirst grew for the man's blood. Within seconds, the vampires had the man surrounded.

But the man stood calm. As the circle of fiends closed in on him, he pulled forth a silver crucifix. Holding it at arm's length, the vampires cowered back and shielded their sight from the cross. The man was able to force them back enough to maneuver him-self so that the wall was to his back, and the creatures were at his front.

The vampires began to whisper back and forth in their tongue. The man couldn't quite hear what they were planning, but it soon became apparent. Two of the creatures picked up chairs. Another picked up a heavy flag pole base that sat in one of the far corners of the room. Smiles and laughs came from the vampires once again.

As the man held up the crucifix, a chair launched through the air suddenly. The man barely ducked out of the way as the chair smashed into the wall behind him with great force. Evil laughs came from the creatures. Another chair whistled through the air, and this time clipped the man in the shoulder before crash-ing into a Christmas tree display. The man tried his best to shake it off and knew he had to think of a way out of this fast as he saw another vampire pick up another chair to throw. The vampire with the heavy flag pole base readied his throw. "You can't hold us back forever!" The two female vampires giggled with delight. "I don't need to," the man replied, using his free hand to reach into his pocket. He pulled a silver embossed lighter set with vampire fangs on either side, out of his pocket. The man flipped the lid and raised it to the low ceiling directly under a sprinkler head. He flicked at the flint wheel with his thumb, and a flame came to life.

Within a couple of seconds, the temperature-sensitive glass

bulb of the sprinkler head burst from the heat of the lighter's flame. In turn, this caused the entire sprinkler system of the building to activate, as the fire alarm began to blare. Water touched everything as the man pocketed his lighter and readied himself for the next series of events that were about to happen. Suddenly deep howls of pain and screams of agony came from each of the creatures. The water immediately began to burn the flesh, hair, and eyes of the vampires like acid. Unbeknown to the group, the man, an ordained minister, came hours earlier and incanted a Holy chant to bless the well water that supplied the building. It was now a shower of acid to them.

All of the vampires dropped to the floor, struggling with the intense pain as they yowled and screeched in torture. Quickly, the man made his move. He reached into his pocket and pulled a short, silver-coated cable saw. He crossed his arms to make a loop. As one of the female vampires lifted to her knees, crying out in pain, the man threw the loop over her head and neck and pulled the two loops he held in each hand. The silver cable blade pulled through, and her body exploded into flames as her head immediately decapitated from her body.

He walked to the other female vampire who was in a heap on the floor. But she ultimately succumbed to the drenching of the Holy water. The vampire's body was in a fetal position, steaming, and the flesh was melting off to expose bones and drenched clothes. In a few moments, the body reduced to nothing more than a puddle of steaming ooze.

The man continued to make his way through the room, stopping momentarily to retrieve his cane from the floor. He pulled the shoe cap off the bottom of the rod to reveal a hollowed shaft. As he walked up to another vampire struggling with the intense pain, the man flipped the cane's end toward the creature. A silver blade slid from the shaft and into the creature's chest. The sword found its mark in the vampire's heart. Immediately, the monster reduced to wet, smoldering ashes within seconds.

There was a sudden crash as a chair smashed through a large

window at the back of the room. The man turned to see the two remaining creatures blindly run and throw themselves through the shattered window into the snow and out of the rain of Holy water.

The two vampires landed a few feet from one another in the snow next to a short hedge of snow-covered evergreen bushes sparsely decorated with twinkling white Christmas lights. The two, still incapacitated from the intense pain, struggled to re-group.

The moonlight broke through the partial clouds illuminating the surroundings with adequate light from the freshly fallen snow.

A back door opened to the building. The two vampires could barely make out a silhouette of a tall figure in a top hat through their blurred vision. The snow crunched under his step as the man walked through the fresh snow. He plucked the top hat from his head and tossed it in the snow between the two wounded creatures. The man stood a few paces from the vampires resetting his grip on his cane. He then removed his shades and placed them in his coat pocket, revealing to the two that his vision was just fine.

"Well, well, well," the man sighed as he sized up the two. "So tell êm, kê sêtetnêo vút master?" (Translated; "So tell me, who is your master?"), the man asked, standing over the severely wounded vampires. " Êtez will tell vedo nú!" (Translated; "We will tell you nothing!"), one of the vampires growled, rubbing his burning eyes. "Oh, no?" the man replied. He bent down to face the vampire. "Do vedo like magic?" the man asked as he reached into his pocket a pulled out a silver dollar coin. "Watch closely." the man said, catching the attention of the two. Their glowing eyes still burned with intense pain, as they watched on...

The man fluttered his hand holding the coin, and within a few misdirecting motions with his other hand, the coin was gone. The two vampires hissed and moaned as they were unimpressed with the man's simple trick. "Oh, didn't like that one? Well, maybe make something a little bigger, disappear?" the man said to one of the vampires. He leaned in and whispered to the other, "Watch this..." The man stood up and glared at the two with an evil grin.

A sudden shrill whistle came from the man's lips as both of the creatures flinched slightly. A moment later, the vampire closest to the hedge cried out in agony. The other vampire looked on in horror as his counterpart rolled to his stomach and begged for the other to help him. The man grinned and looked directly into the scared eyes of the creature as his companion howled in pain. "And I say the magic word.." The man waited a moment. "Twilight!" Suddenly, the screaming vampire was yanked through to the other side of the hedge in one mighty pull. The creature's claw marks were left in the snow, deep enough that frozen dirt turned from its struggle to hold on. A few seconds later, a gruesome scream, then a crunch and a fireball ignited and dimmed, then quiet...

The last vampire sat in shock and looked up at the man. "So, here we are," the man said, tapping the snowpack from his boot with his cane. "I'm going to ask you again... Kê sêtetnêo vedo master?" (Translated; "Who is your Master?") "What if I don't tell you? Are you going to make me disappear too?" the vampire asked, trying to buy time. "No," the man replied, as a sudden rustle came from the nearby hedge and caught the vampire's attention.

A bulky, fury figure of a large dog emerged, stealthily walking past the man and stopped inches from the creature. The vampire cowered back into the snow as the massive German Shepherd shook his coat free of the wet snow. The dog raised the hair on its back, baring its silver fangs to the creature. "I won't make you disappear, but he will," The man said as the dog began to growl.

The vampire sat frozen, locking eyes with the K9 as the dog's crucifix charm hanging from its collar, slightly twirled, catching the dim light. "This is Zed. And between you and me, he's about half as patient as I am. And he hasn't eaten yet. So he's a little, "Bah Humbug!" at the moment. So, I'll ask you one more time. Who is your Master?"

Once more, the defiant vampire sneered at the man's question, but only for a moment. "Zed," the man said. The Shepherd suddenly stomped and snarled at the creature. The vampire cowered back, immediately answering, "Delgado!" The man stood motionless for a moment. The name made him cringe with rage. He then placed his cane against a nearby shrub. Suddenly with a fluid motion, the man kneeled to the creature and pulled a silver blade to its neck. The man leaned in close, inches from the vampire's twisted pale face. "What did you say?" The man asked calmly and clearly, waiting for an answer. "D...Delgado... Victor Delgado. Please..." A tear rolled down the creature's cold-skinned cheek. "And where is he?" the man asked, holding the blade steady and tight to the fiend's neck. "Far from here.. He keeps on the move."

The man's attention was suddenly drawn to the distant sound of sirens. "And your name?" the man asked, turning his focus back onto the cowering vampire.

"It's Malcolm." "Well, Malcolm, I want you to deliver a message to Victor. Can you do that?" The vampire nervously nodded. "Good," the man said, as he grabbed a fist full of Malcolm's burnt hair, holding his head still. With the precision of a surgeon, the man pulled the silver blade to Malcolm's bare forehead. He then began to carve the initials, J.B., as the vampire screamed in agony. The creature's skin burned as the silver blade etched a permanent scar onto Malcolm's high forehead.

"You tell your Master, Victor, that John Bishop is coming for him. John released his grip on the tuft of hair and pushed Malcolm back to the snow-covered ground. The vampire shuddered from the intense pain as John stood to his feet and Zed backed up and twirled to John's side.

"Malcolm, you can go now. And Merry Christmas." John said as he retrieved his cane from the nearby shrub. Solemnly, Malcolm slowly rose to his feet and bowed to John, knowing that his existence had been spared. Still very weak, the vampire quietly faded into the darkness..

Within a few minutes, a black jeep drove up the main road as two local police cars and a fire truck pulled into the crowded Legion parking lot sirens blaring and lights flashing...

Chapter Two

Two weeks earlier...

The local County plow truck made a slow pass down the road, which led into the Creekwood Middle School. The parking lot was full of both faculty and staff vehicles after a two-day shutdown from a quick winter storm. But the foothills town was used to regular blasts of winter this time of year.

With two days off, and but just a week and a half away from Christmas break, the teachers' jobs were more difficult than usual, as the students were eager to begin their two weeks and then some, vacation.

Class was just about to begin as the morning sunshine glistened off the wind-sculpted drifts in the fields surrounding the building.

A well-groomed man dressed in a gray wool herringbone blazer carrying a black Samsonite Omega Gl briefcase made his way down the empty hall as he reached just outside the classroom door.

As he entered the room, chaos ensued, students out of their seats, talking and screaming simultaneously, as other students were isolated by their Walkman headphones blaring their favorite tunes. A few other misfit students were in random groups, some sitting on the noisy heater at the back wall of the classroom warming their bums. A few others gathered at a desk, playing Dungeons and Dragons, rolling multiple-sided dice, and flipping through a D & D Monster manual. The man went nearly unnoticed as he calmly walked to the front of the class and placed his briefcase on the cluttered desk.

The man scanned the classroom of chaos with his one eye, his left eye covered with an eye patch. Clearing his throat, the man said, "Ok, class," but no response. "Class," the man said louder, still no response. With this, the man turned to the chalkboard behind him. Forming his hand into a claw, he made sure that only the tips of his groomed nails touched the surface of the board. Slowly, the man began to drag his nails firmly across the board. A piercing and continuous tone filled the classroom. Slow but sure, the sound began to catch the attention of each student. Some clasped their ears with their hands, others winced and cringed as the agonizing sound continued and intensified. Suddenly the classroom was silent. The man slowly turned to face the crowd with an evil grin. "Ok, class, please take your seats." With the man's words, the students began to fall into their seats, abandon their groups, and place their games, toys, and music makers into their desks.

Within a few moments, the class focused not so much on the man, but more so, on his eye patch. Giggles ensued as the man once again turned to face the chalkboard with a piece of chalk in hand. "Good morning, class. My name is Mr. Bishop." The chalk clicked at each letter he wrote. "But you can call me Mr. B., and I will be filling in for Mrs. Summers while she's on maternity leave." John placed the chalk into the rail tray and turned to face the class. He glanced down at the teacher's desk and scanned Mrs. Summer's weekly planner. She was very meticulous and had her lesson itinerary written out months in advance. The current subject was Greek Mythology, and it couldn't have been more appropriate.

"So class, I understand the Principal was just in and took roll call, and all of us are here, so let's get started." Briefed minutes earlier by Principal Harker, he told John the class was generally a good group of kids, but they were a bit "unruly" at times. But John was up to the task. He thought of an excellent lead-in to grasp the attention of the class.

"Greek Mythology. Ok, class. Let's open your texts to Chapter Two." There was a sudden scramble and rustling of pages of textbooks as the students reluctantly turned to the appropriate chapter. "Alright, chapter two, the characters of Greek Mythology." John read from his text, "You should all enjoy this chapter." he commented.

"You know a lot about this stupid stuff?" A student in the front row asked. John looked up at the boy as giggles and moans of agreement came from other random students. "Well, sure," John said, calmly walking toward the boy's desk. He saw the Dungeons and Dragons Monster Manual peeking out from under a short stack of books on the corner of the boy's desk. "So, you play D & D?" John asked the boy. The boy looked down at his books as John pulled the Monster Manual to the surface. "What's your name," John asked. "Mark," the boy replied, reaching for the book as John handed it to him. "Ok, Mark. I want you to flip to the

"M's" in your book. The rest of the class became intrigued. Mark turned to the "M's" in the manual. "Start turning the pages," John said.

The boy began to flip through slowly, page by page. John stopped him, pointing to a page. "Who's this?" The boy looked down. "Medusa." John smiled. "Ok, keep turning." The boy continued working his nimble fingers on the crisp pages. "Stop, what's that?" John asked. The boy again looked down at the book. "Minotaur," Mark said. "Both of these are from guess what?" John asked with a smile. "Greek Mythology?" Mark asked, surprised. "You got it!" John said. "Cyclops is in there, and also Greek Mythology." John continued. "Anyone ever hear of a superhero named Wonder Woman?" Twelve random students raised their hands. "She was what?" John asked. "An Amazon?" A girl from the back blurted out. "Correct!" John said. "A tribe of women from Greek Mythology."

John turned and again walked to the front of the room. All eyes were on him. "So you see class, Greek Mythology is all around us. It's in our everyday lives and activities." John turned to face the kids, all hanging on his words.

He looked over to a boy, sitting at a desk by the window, bundled up in an oversized printed hoodie. "What's your name?" John asked. "Eddie," the boy said quietly. "Eddie, stand up for a second," John said, walking toward the boy. Reluctantly, the boy slowly scooted in his seat, screeching his desk across the floor slightly, and stood up. John reached down and picked up a new No. 2 pencil off a nearby student's desk. Using it as a pointer, John took the pencil and tapped at the front of the boy's garment. It was a printed movie sweatshirt of *The Monster Squad.* "Werewolves... Witches... Vampires..." John said, monotone, smiling. "Greek Mythology," he added, pointing the pencil at the classic monster line-up on the boy's hoodie.

"Vampires?" A voice stuttered from across the classroom. "No way," the student added. "Gottcha!" John thought. "Vampires, yes! Greek Mythology," John said as he motioned for Eddie to take his seat once again.

"Actually, one of the very first mentions of a vampire may be traced to Greek Mythology in the story of a young Italian man named Ambrogio and love of his life, Selena." John, once again, fascinating the class with his words as he continued... "And long story short, a series of blessings and curses from the Gods, transformed this young man into history's first vampire."

"What about Dracula?" a student commented from the back. "What about Dracula?" John asked the student. "Well, I thought he was the first vampire." the student added. "No, but I guess you could say that Count Dracula was the first vampire to be glorified by Hollywood," John remarked to the student with a smile.

"Class, let's talk about "vampires" for a moment." John took his place, once again, at the front of the class. He picked up a stick of worn chalk and wrote, "Vampires" in gothic-style letters on the board. He then wrote two headings. "Strengths" and "Weaknesses."

"Ok, so what do we know about vampires?" John asked, turning from the board and scanning the class for answers. "They're strong," one student remarked. "And fast," another added. "You're both right," John said. "A vampire is as strong as ten men," John said, writing the remark under the "Strengths" on the board. "And a vampire can move like the wind," John commented, adding it to the same column. "So never expect to win a physical fight against a vampire and never try to outrun one." John turned to the class. "And when you do run, it makes your heart pump faster and makes your blood warmer." In his best mock Dracula voice, John added, "And it makes a vampire all the more eager to suck your blood! Blahhhh!" All the students began to laugh and giggle at John's remark.

"Ok, so what else do we know?" John waited for a moment. "No reflection?" A shy student answered from the front row. "That's right, no reflection. And no breath when it's cold." John added, looking outside at the cold snow.

"What else?" John asked, glancing at the classroom clock. "Can't they hypnotize?" A student asked as she leaned back in her seat. "Yes, very good," John said as he made his way back to the board. "A vampire has the ability to influence people, especially weak-minded people with hypnosis, and can also read minds." John writes "hypnosis" under the list of "strengths."

"They can fly," Eddie added. "Yes, Ed. They can fly, float in the air, crawl on walls and ceilings." John added it to the list as he spoke. "And vampires can do all of these things because they are what?" John asked, placing the chalk in the tray. "Because they're freaks!" A student answered as the room filled with laughter. John smiled. "Because they're immortal," Mark said, looking at John. The laughter subsided. "Exactly, Mark. A vampire is immortal."

"So class, let's assume an army of vampires is trying to take over the town. An army of immortals that have all these strengths. How do we stand a chance against them?" John glanced around the room as the students thought about his scenario.

"So, what is a weakness of the vampire?" John asked the class. "The sun," a student answered. "There's one, sunlight." John said as he picked up the chalk and wrote it under the "Weaknesses" column. "During the day, you would pretty much be safe. Vampires hate the sun. Sunlight will destroy them," John said, facing the class once again. "What else?" "Crosses," an answer from the back row. "Yes, a cross or crucifix will push a vampire away from you, but..." John scanned the class room intently and continued. "For this to work, you have to have complete faith! If not, a vampire will not be affected in any way and attack you." John tries very hard to make this very clear to the students.

"Ok, another weakness?" "Water," a student mumbles. "Holy water, yes. It will burn a vampire like acid," John said as he wrote it on the board. "But, it must be blessed water." "That'd be cool, a squirt gun with holy water in it." The class clown responded with laughter from his fellow classmates. John laughed as well, but considered it a great idea.

"Another weakness?" John waited for another response from the class. "A stake in the heart," a student commented through the silence. "Yep! But this is best done when a vampire is at rest. I don't recommend running up to a vampire and attempting to stab it in the chest. You probably won't get that far," John added with a smile. "Yeah, only when he's in his coffin sleeping," a student added. "Well, first of all, that's a Hollywood gimmick for the most part. A vampire doesn't always sleep or rest in a coffin. Any dark place- basements, caves, under a pile of dirt, a few may be found in caskets. But they could be found in any dark place," John said, enjoying the conversation. "Another weakness?" A few moments later, another answer came. "Garlic?" "Yes, cloves of garlic. Not really a weapon, but vampires despise the smell. So if you have garlic hanging around, they will be less tempted," John added.

"Anything else we know that could help fight vampires?" John asked once again. "They can't come in, unless you let them in," a student said from the back. "By invitation only, correct," John continued. "This is a true myth that a vampire cannot enter into someone's home without being invited in. They will not cross the door's threshold until you tell them that they are welcomed. But they can enter any public place or business with no problem," John explained, as he wrote, "By invitation only" on the board. "So you may be safest at home, with the curtains pulled, shades down, and doors locked," John added.

"Any more?" John asked, waiting patiently. "What about silver?" a student asked from the front row. "Yes, silver can be used as a weapon, such as a blade, knife, or sword," John said. "A silver bullet!" A student blurted, confident in his answer. "That's used to kill a werewolf dumbass," another student added, receiving laughter from the class. "Well, technically, you probably could kill a vampire with a silver bullet, but they move so fast that when you fire the gun, they would simply sidestep the bullet. Then they would get you," John said with a smile. "But, silver to a vampire is like poison and will hurt them and kill them if the wound is severe enough. If you're lucky enough to stab or cut one with a silver blade, that is," John added.

"Ok, let's get one more," John said as he finished writing "Silver" on the board. "What about fire?" a shy girl asked quietly. "Fire, yes. Fire will kill anything. But vampires can withstand fire for a short time. And if they are able to escape the flames or put themselves out, they may be able to regenerate and heal themselves. Very good," John said as the girl smiled with confidence.

"Well, now we have some excellent information to help us deal with the vampire infestation when the town gets attacked," John said jokingly. The students began to laugh at the notion as the class bell began to blare. "Ok, class, read chapter three, and we'll discuss it on Monday," John said through the commotion as the students raced toward the classroom door for lunch.

John turned to the board and knew he had given the class a plethora of basic but useful information to keep them alive as he knew the town might be in trouble with the aforementioned subject matter.

"Excuse me, Mr. B." John turned to face a short-haired blonde girl, dressed in a colorful, yet coordinated outfit. She was clutching a short stack of glamour magazines to her stomach, chewing on a wad of gum. "Yes." John acknowledged the student. "Can I ask you a question?" She asked in a serious tone. "Absolutely," John answered, rubbing his hands free of chalk dusk.

"Well, this may sound stupid, but do you believe that vampires like really exist?" the girl asked.

John crossed his arms and could see the girl was focused on his answer. "What's your name, dear?" "Anne, but my friends call me Buffy," the girl responded, popping a bubble from her gum." "I do, why do you ask?" John replied, a little surprised at the girl's curiosity. "I do too! Like, I think I've seen a few around here," Anne said, looking down at the floor. "You mean here, in town?" John asked calmly. "Yeah, at night, I see them, like around," Anne replied, twirling her blonde locks with her free hand. "Are you afraid?" John asked, showing concern. The girl looked up with a smile and tilted her head thinking for a moment. "No. Like for some reason, I think they are afraid of me." John smiled. "Well, that's good because they feed on fear. A vampire can smell it! But they can be frightened just as easily as a person. So why do you think they are afraid of you?" John asked, intrigued by the girl. "Well, like, I've had these far-out dreams where I am fighting them, and like I know exactly what to do and how to kill them. It's like weird! And not once am I scared. And I like... Enjoy it!" The girl smiled, wickedly at the thought "And oh, I like saw one outside my window the other night, and we like locked eyes, and her's were like glowing, it was sooo cool!"

The girl's words began to ramble together as she got more excited, telling John the story. But John did his best to decipher her words as she continued... "Like she looked at me, and I could read her mind. At first, it freaked me out, because I could feel her trying to read my thoughts, but then I was like, "No!" and then she couldn't. But then I was able to see and hear her thoughts. Then, she like got nervous and backed away and she looked scared of me. And I could feel her fear. She like knew- I would kill her!"

John leaned back, taking it all in. "Wow," he sighed. "So, what else happened?" Anne looked at John and continued, calming down slightly. "There's a group of them, eight of them, two women and six men, planning an attack." John carefully began to put to memory the girl's words. "Anne, where and when? Do you know?" John asked. The girl thought calmly for a moment then nodded at John. "Yeah, at the Legion. At the Christmas party. Oh my God, what should I do, I need to do something!" Anne became excited at the thought, as if she could see what was to happen.

John clasped her shoulders gently and captured her attention as she calmed down. He looked in her eyes and smiled. "Anne, you already have. You don't need to do anything else. You told me, and that's all you had to do. Everything will be fine." The girl looked up at John. "But Mr. B, I can help, I know I can!" "I know you can too, but your time will come soon enough, Anne." John released his grip and stepped to the desk to gather his briefcase.

"And who knows, before you know it, people may refer to you as "Buffy," the vampire slayer." Both Anne and John laughed at the notion. "You better get to lunch and get a bite to eat before your next class, Anne," John said as he grabbed his keys from the cluttered desk. "Mr. B., can I ask you one more question?" Anne asked as she walked toward the door to the hall. "Sure," John said, following behind. "The eye patch, what happened to your eye?" Anne asked, looking up at John. Reaching up, John lifted the patch to reveal his eye to Anne. "It's an old pirate trick. Keep it covered, so it's always adjusted for darkness when I go vampire hunting!" John winked at Anne as he dropped the eye patch back into place. Anne smiled as the two walked into the hall...

Hours later, a black jeep pulled into a roadside hotel off of the highway. The early evening air was crisp as the sun was setting. John parked the jeep and exited the vehicle. He turned and collected his briefcase from the passenger seat. He closed and locked the door to the jeep and walked past the hotel office, waiving to the manager on duty through the window. Suddenly realizing it was John, the manager motioned for him to come into the office.

John turned and walked through the covered entrance and entered a side door into the main lobby. "Hey John, I almost forgot, I have a message for you." The man turned to retrieve a folded piece of paper from a mail slot for John's room. "It just came this afternoon. One of the office staff took a call from someone looking to speak with you. Here you go."

John reached over the counter and pulled the paper from the man's grasp. "Thanks, Tony, appreciate it." "Not a problem," the man replied. "So, what's the special on the dinner menu tonight?" John asked, glancing at the message in his hand. "Meatloaf and potatoes," the man answered. "Yummy!" John said, facetiously with a smile. "Hey, it's not that bad!" Tony said with a laugh. "Oh, I just took Zed back to your room about twenty minutes ago. He spent most of the day in the office with me," he added. "Thanks again, Tony," John said, raising the paper in the air to the man as he walked back outside. Folding the message, John placed it in his coat pocket and walked across the snow-packed lot to his room.

As John juggled the keys in his hand, there was a thump and a short bark from within the room. John unlocked and opened the door. Zed excitedly met John at the door, prancing and whining as John walked into the room and closed the door to the cold outside.

Inside, John flipped a switch on the wall, and two bedside

lamps illuminated the room. Zed stood on his hind legs and gently placed his front paws on John's chest. Putting down his briefcase in a chair slightly pulled out from under a nearby table, John clasped Zed's floppy head and scratched behind the K9's ears. "How you doing, bud?" John asked as Zed flopped his head under John's moving hands and panted with joy. "Ok, ok, bud, here's a cookie," John said, reaching into his coat pocket. He smashed the doggie biscuit into Zed's muzzle, and the dog chomped with delight.

Zed dropped to the floor, turned and leapt onto the closest bed to get comfortable as John placed his keys onto the dresser. The T.V. was already on as it kept Zed occupied when he was by himself.

"We'll get a bite to eat in a little while, bud," John said as Zed licked his chops and laid his head down on the fresh linens. John walked over and removed his coat, pulling the folded message from the pocket. He tossed the jacket onto a nearby chair and plopped down onto the bed next to the nightstand.

He unfolded the paper and read the message to himself. John smiled and reached over, pulling the rotor phone onto the bed next to him and lifted the receiver. His nimble fingers began to dial as he glanced back at the paper for the rest of the phone number. John could hear the phone ringing as his eyes focused on the T.V.

Moments later, someone answered the phone on the other end. Zed glanced over at John as he spoke on the phone. "Hey, it's John. How are you?... I'm good, Zed's good. So what's up?... Wow, really?... Yep, we sure do... Yeah, I'm sure it would be worth the trip... Well, I'll tell you what. I have a few things to tie up here, and a Christmas party to crash. But afterward, we'll be on our way... Sure, you got it!... We'll see you in a week or so... Yeah, you too... Ok, bye."

Intently, Zed watched as John hung up the receiver and placed the phone back onto the nightstand. John got up from the bed and tossed the unfolded paper to the table. "Well, Zed, it looks like we're going to have to return to the scene of the crime." Zed lifted and tilted his head to John's words as he watched John began to undress on his way into the bathroom to take a hot shower before dinner...

Return to Dyer

Chapter Three

I t was mid-morning as the black jeep rolled back through town from the local hospital. Zed sat poised in the passenger seat as some Van Halen pumped through the speakers. John counted the new storefronts and buildings, now constructed and open for business in Dyer.

A grand opening was underway for a new Blockbuster on a busy corner as a McDonald's drive-thru lined with waiting cars. As John drove through downtown Dyer, the empty buildings were slowly coming back to life with activity.

An electrician was putting the finishing touches on a new neon RadioShack sign as numerous "opening soon" posters lined the windows of the vacant buildings. It was apparent that a new life had come to Dyer.

John smiled as he turned down a new crossroad that was named "Bishop" and "Zed" street. A short drive brought the jeep to a renovated building of new apartments. John pulled into the parking lot and scanned the apt. number on the card that he received at the hospital from one of the nurses.

John exited the vehicle, and Zed leapt from the seat and onto the ground next to him. "Come on, bud, let's see if we can find her," John said as he slammed the door and pocketed his keys. Zed barked with delight as the two walked toward the building's entrance.

Moments later, an elevator door opened, as John and Zed

emerged and walked down the wide hall. The smell of fresh paint and the newly installed carpet was evident to the nose. Halfway down the hall, the two turned and stood at the door of apt. 7C.

John knocked as Zed sat next to him on the floor, facing the door. From inside, there was a sound of commotion and then quiet. John could see the light from the peep-hole became dark. Then suddenly, the sound of door locks fumbled with excitedly.

The door flew open, and there stood Kate, wide-eyed, damp haired, dressed in her nursing scrubs with a big smile on her face. "Oh my God, John, what are you doing here?" Her voice cracked with excitement. Without thinking, Kate rushed out of the door and embraced John tightly. "Hey Kate," John replied, wincing in pain as he tried his best not to show it. Kate released her embrace and looked down at Zed. "Zed, how are you, boy!" She bent down and rubbed the K9's head as Zed licked her face excitedly. Kate laughed with delight. "Come in, what a surprise!" She stepped back in as John and Zed followed, closing the door behind them.

Kate continued to smile from ear to ear. "So, what brings you back to Dyer?" "Well, I got a call from Preacher Bob, and he found something he wanted me to see," John said. "Oh," Kate sighed as her face fell slightly from John's answer. "I went to the hospital to see you, and they told me you weren't there yet. And Lisa gave me your address after I told her who I was. "Oh yeah, well, what's up?" Kate asked, slightly shaking off her disappointment.

"Well, I need a little medical attention," John said with a slight smile. "Ok, well, what can I do?" Kate asked, looking John up and down for signs of injury. Carefully, John turned and began to remove his black leather coat. Wincing, he nimbly pulled his left arm from the sleeve. Kate took his coat as John started to unbutton his shirt. Kate went behind John and helped him to remove the garment carefully. She knew something was wrong as John moaned in pain.

Kate came to John's front with his shirt in hand and saw the reason for his pain. "My God, John! What did you do?" Kate asked,

36

shocked at his injury. John's left shoulder, severely bruised and clearly popped out of place. "I got into a furniture fight with a bunch of vampires," John said with a smile. Kate shook her head, "You know how ridiculous that would sound coming from someone else?" Kate sighed, "What am I going to do with you?" John looked into her eyes and smiled. "Here, sit," Kate said, pulling over a chair from a small dinette set.

John took a seat on the chair as Kate looked his shoulder over. "Oh, John," she said with a sigh. "Ok, let's see what we can do." Kate reached down and slightly spread John's knees apart. "Kate, what are you..." John mumbled as she carefully straddled John's left knee and gently took a seat. "Just relax." Kate smiled as John tried to compose himself as she sat in closer to him.

Facing John, Kate carefully grasped his left arm and shoulder and caressed them softly. "Now, just relax, let your arm hang loose, and don't try to fight me," Kate said seductively, looking into John's uncovered eye. She slowly leaned in closer as the radio played the Righteous Brother's, "Unchained Melody" in the background.

Zed sat and tilted his head, watching as John became more uncomfortable and excited at the same time at Kate's actions. Moving in closer, Kate continued to keep John guessing and thinking about what she was going to do next. "Does this hurt?" Kate asked in a sultry tone, as she lifted his arm softly. "No," John gulped with anticipation. With a seductive look and but just inches from kissing John on the lips, Kate whispered, "Are you ready?" Zed, whimpered slightly on the floor and covered his muzzle with his paw. John nervously nodded with a shaky, "Yes."

With one fluid motion, Kate turned, pulled, lifted, and pushed with both hands, as three loud "pops" came from John's shoulder. He hardly winced as Kate leaned in and set her cheek to his and blew softly in his ear. "How's that, better?" she whispered. "Oh yeah," John sighed, feeling goose bumps all over his body. "Good," Kate whispered. "Still wearing that eye patch, I see," she added as she gently lifted the patch from John's left eye. He closed his eye as Kate gave him a soft kiss on his eyelid. "I always thought that eye patch made you look sexy," Kate whispered, with a subtle smile. Sliding the patch back into place, Kate pulled away and slowly, slid off of John's knee. "You've got a healer's touch, Kate," John added, moving his stiff shoulder slightly.

"You can get up now, we're done," Kate said with a playful smile as she stood in front of John. "Uh, I think I'll sit here for a minute," John said, glancing down at the bulge in his pants. Kate laughed under her breath as she knew she was successful in her attempt to get a "rise" out of John.

A few minutes later, the door to Kate's apartment opened to the hallway, and John and Zed emerged. John turned to face Kate as she stood in the open doorway. Zed took a seat and sat patiently. "Well, it was good to see you, John. I missed you and Zed." Kate said as she reached down and scratched the side of Zed's muzzle. "Kate, are you sure you can't come with us to see what Preacher Bob found?" John asked. "Well, I would, but I have to get to work. You two go on ahead." Kate said with a smile, looking down at the floor then back to John. "So, will you be staying in town a while then?" "We may stay a few days, not quite sure yet, but we'll see," John answered. "Oh, ok. Well, maybe I'll see you two around then?" Kate asked. "Maybe," John replied. "Ok, well, maybe I'll see you then. Bye." Kate said, backing inside and slowly closing the door. "Kate!" John mustered. Kate quickly pulled the door open with a smile. "Yes?" John leaned in slightly, resting on the doorframe. "I... I, uh, just wanted to thank you for fixing my shoulder." Kate's face fell slightly, "Oh, you're welcome, John, anytime." Zed sat quietly, looking up at John. "Ok, then. Bye." John said, pushing himself away from the door. "Bye," Kate said once again, closing the door.

"Ok, bud, let's get going," John said to Zed as he turned and began to walk away. Zed continued to sit by the door, looking at John quietly. After a few paces, John noticed Zed was not coming. "Zed, let's go. Now." John motioned for the K9 to follow. Zed just sat quietly, looking at John over his shoulder. "Zed, now!" John said, becoming frustrated at the dog's defiance.

Zed sat his ground, his pitiful gaze drilled right into John. With a deep sigh, John began to walk back. "Ok, ok!" John looked down at Zed and knocked on the door. "Sometimes, you're a pain in my ass!" John mumbled as he collected his emotions. Zed still, sat quietly looking at John with a slight bearing of his silver fangs as if smiling.

A clatter came from behind the door, and it slowly opened once again. Kate stood silent with a smirk on her face looking at John. "Uh, I almost forgot," John said, looking down at Zed. "I know you're busy, but I was wondering, if you had some free time, maybe we could get some dinner or a cup of coffee or something?" John muddled through, his face turned bright red.

Kate walked out into the hall, softly closing the door behind her. "John Bishop, are you asking me out on a date?" Kate smile at John at the joy of watching his squirm. John looked down at Zed as the dog calmly looked back. "Well, no, I mean, if you'd like, yes." John stuttered. Kate leaned in and palmed John's cheek in her hand. "I'd love to John. How about picking me up around eight tonight?" John calmed from her warm touch and smiled. "Ok then, I'll see you around eight." "Ok," Kate whispered, smiling at John. She opened the door, walked back in, and softly closed the door.

John took a deep breath of relief and looked down at Zed. "Ok, satisfied now? Can we go?" Content, Zed quietly barked, stood up and pranced down the hall toward the elevator as John followed behind, shaking his head...

The Greater Dyer Church of Bob

Chapter Four

I t was early afternoon, and the sun was high, though it was still a chilly winter day, although much warmer than it was in Creekwood. It was unseasonably warm in Dyer with no snow whatsoever for the upcoming holiday. Though, it didn't seem to put a damper on the holiday spirits of the townsfolk that were out and about.

A black jeep slowed and turned off the main highway onto the newly paved road that led into the Dyer cemetery. Moments later, John and Zed pulled into the parking lot of a beautiful new building that was to be the "Greater Dyer Church of God," as it was on the newly constructed sign at the edge of the lot.

John parked the jeep next to a white electrician van and a loaded down, rusted, long bed, Ford pick-up, more than likely belonging to a contractor. John and Zed jumped from the vehicle and walked side by side toward the entrance to the building.

As they approached, the sounds of construction work could be heard coming from inside the propped-open door. John glanced over at a nearby designated parking spot marked with a sign that read, "Clergy Parking Only." In front of the sign, sat a new shiny black Lincoln Mark VII with a personalized license plate, which read, "Prchr Bob." John smiled as they reached the door.

As John and Zed walked through the door, they followed a narrow path that meandered between buckets, tools, scraps of wood, paneling, and sheetrock. A few people were inside, rushing about, each working on finishing an assigned job before the day's end.

John and Zed cleared the construction area, and their ears honed in on a familiar voice. It was the unmistakable, heavy Southern accent of Preacher Bob arguing with someone over the phone.

Zed's ears perked as he began to trot around a corner and down a short hall. John followed a few paces behind as he saw Zed walk through an open door from the hallway. A few seconds later, Preacher Bob's angry voice turned into a playful and welcoming tone as laughter followed.

"Ok, ok, then. We'll push the install to next week then. But I ain't too happy about it!" Bob mumbled on the phone, as he playfully tried to fight Zed, muzzling him with a wet nose and licking his hand excitedly.

Hanging up the phone receiver, Bob turned his full attention to Zed. "Hey, how are you, Brother Zed?" Preacher asked, dropping to the floor to meet the K9. Zed rolled onto his back and kicked wildly as Preacher roughly rubbed on his tummy and chest.

"Well, look at you two," John said, standing at the door, crossing his arms, enjoying the spectacle. "Brother, John!" Preacher said, clumsily working his way to his feet with a laugh as Zed fought to hold his attention. "Nice to see you too, Bob," John said, reaching out with an outstretched hand. "We are Brothers, not acquaintances, John." Preacher Bob said, grasping John's open palm and pulling him close into a tight embrace.

"So how are you?" Preacher asked, patting John on the back with excitement. "I'm good! And from the looks of things, you're exceptionally well yourself," John said, smiling, holding Preacher by both shoulders. "God has graced me, and Dyer, all thanks to you and Zed," Preacher said gracefully, smiling back at John. "So let me show you around our new church, Brother John." The three turned and walked out into the hall.

As John and Zed followed Preacher Bob into the central atrium of the church, he continued. "Welcome Brother John and Zed to the new Greater Dyer Church of God!" Preacher Bob turned to face the two and raised his arms to the proclamation. Zed broke left and John to the right of Preacher as they both walked around him to admire the building.

A large circular vaulted ceiling, encased with curved skylights, illuminated the area with a natural light. It was dispersed by a large tilted cross of weathered wood, which spanned the center, left and right of the open ceiling. On either side of the outer walls, four large stained-glass windows captured the sunlight and bathed the room in a rainbow of soothing colors. Three sections of pews, set in a half-circle, tiered downward toward the round stage at the front of the church.

"The building, designed to be acoustically sound. No outside sound can enter, and from the stage, my voice reaches everyone in attendance," Preacher Bob boasted as John and Zed admired the artistry of the building's design. "The skylights offer natural lighting and supplemental heat in the winter months, saving on energy costs. Many of the pews were donated and refinished and believe it or not, one of the stained glass windows survived the fire. That- and the cross on stage," Preacher Bob added, pointing to a window and then to the charred cross hanging at the back center of the stage. "Two links to the original church. And we came in under budget!" Preacher added proudly.

"Wow, impressive," John commented, nodding slightly. "And my parish is up to 225 people and growing steadily!" Bob said with a confident tone. "We still have a few issues to work out and things to finish up, but we are a working house of the Lord!"

Preacher Bob, placing his hands behind his back, took a few steps toward John. "So, are you ready to see what we found that might interest you?" John turned and looked at Preacher with a smile. "You bet I am." Preacher smiled, "Come with me, Brother." With that, Bob led John and Zed back down the hall to a locked door.

"The demolition crew found a small chamber in one of the corners of the cellar. There were three large stones cemented in place in the wall." Preacher fumbled with his set of keys as he continued. "When they popped the rocks loose, they stopped and came and got me." Preacher inserted the key to the lock and gave it a turn as the door opened to a small storage room. Preacher flipped on the light and walked to a shelving unit at the back of the room. John and Zed followed behind.

"So I got a flashlight and looked inside the wall, and found this." Carefully, Preacher pulled a small wooden chest bound with rusted iron straps. He placed it on a nearby table for John to examine. It was small but ruggedly built. The wood was slightly discolored and had surface mold, though it was still solid. The iron straps riveted around the thick slats had surface rust but were still intact. The chest was ancient, though very well constructed and built to last. There were two hinged handles on either side with corked hand grips. "My oh my," John whispered, "Preacher, what did you find?" Preacher shook his head, "I don't know. I was hoping you could tell me. And when word got around about what we found, the town's Historical Society wanted to put it in their new museum. Fortunately, I'm not only on the board, but I'm also the Chairman. So I was able to retain it for "further study." Preacher added with a smile.

John turned the front of the chest to the light. There was a small keyhole to what looked to be an intricate lock. "Well, let's give it a try, shall we?" John said as he pulled the iron key from his pocket that Zed found in Lucas's stuffed doll.

The key fit in the lock perfectly. John slightly smiled at Preacher. John took a breath of anticipation and gave the key a turn. John was expecting the lock mechanism to be stiff from age. Though unexpectedly, the lock clicked, and the tumblers turned with little effort. John smiled as Preacher laughed with delight and clapped his hands together.

John stood back slightly, knowing some chests like this one often came equipped with small booby traps that would be triggered when opened or tampered with. John carefully held both sides of the lid and lifted it open slowly. No traps triggered.

Inside the chest, delicately lined with fine silk, the inside of the lid had a solid panel of aromatic cedar. John stepped forward to examine its contents. He reached in and pulled out a thick rectangle object, also carefully wrapped in a silk slip. He placed the bundle on the table gently. John began to pull the flaps of fabric back one by one until the object uncovered.

It was a large book. Bound front to back in a thick hide or skin. "What in God's name is that, leather?" Preacher asked, moving in to take a closer look. John ran his finger along the cover, "I don't know," he replied. John could see and feel words or symbols etched into the surface of the book. It was definitely in a Vampyric text. John knew the language, though written text and symbols were somewhat new to him.

John opened the front cover and began to flip through the book. The pages were a variety of different types of parchment. Some were illustrations, diagrams, journal entries, and footnotes. Some written in black ink, others seemed inked in blood. The second half of the thick book appeared to be the likes of a bible of sorts. Although strange to John, some of the chapters seemed to be missing. John knew this book was a significant find, but to decipher it, was the next challenge.

"Can you make out any of it, Brother John," Bob asked. "A few things here and there... But it's a very ancient language and text. It dates back to the 31st century B.C. The first part of the book seems more recent, maybe from the 17th century. But wow, I believe this is the Vampyric Bible, often referred to as the Old Unholy Testament." John added. "The information in this could change everything," John whispered.

Pulling his attention away, John went back to the open chest. Looking down in the corner, he saw what appeared to be a ring. Reaching in, he plucked the ring up between his fingers and pulled it into the light.

It was gaudy, heavy, and John knew it was gold. A red ruby was set in its center, surrounded by a few black onyx stones and what looked like two rough-cut diamonds.

On one side of the ring was an intricate, engraved "D." On the opposite side, a Vampyric symbol that John recognized as meaning "Lord of Blood and Darkness." Though John was sure, this ring was not the property of Lucas Barlos. Perhaps he had stolen the ring from its rightful owner.

John twirled the ring in his hand until it reached his thumb. The gold band slid over it with ease. John and Preacher looked at each other in disbelief. "Well, it definitely didn't belong to Barlos. But I'd hate to see who it does belong to." John whispered as Preacher nodded his head in agreement. John sat the ring on the corner of the table and went back to the chest.

"Anything else in there, Brother?" Preacher asked. John looked closely in the chest and shook his head. "Nope. That's it." "Well, that's something," Preacher said, picking up the ring and examining it closer. "Wait a minute..." John mumbled as something caught his eye. "What is it," Bob asked, intrigued.

John stood back and eyed the chest. Then he looked inside of it once again. "This chest doesn't look right. It's disproportioned." "What do you mean Brother," Preacher asked as he scratched Zed behind the ears. "Well, it looks deep from the outside. But then you look inside, and it seems too shallow." John said as he reached down into the chest and felt at the bottom of the silk lining. He could feel a rough grain of wood just under the material. John made a knuckle and tapped around the inside bottom of the chest. It sounded solid along the edges, and hollow toward the center.

"Hmmm," John muttered, pulling a sharp, silver stiletto blade seemingly out of mid-air. "How do you do that," Preacher asked, amazed at John's hand speed. "A lot of practice," John replied with a smile. With the skill of a surgeon, John plunged the blade into a crease in the delicate fabric. Cutting the material at an angle, John was able to flip the fabric to the corners of the chest bottom. As quickly as he pulled it, the blade disappeared from sight. Preacher stood amazed at John's hand-eye coordination.

At the inside bottom of the chest was a small iron plate with two latches on either side. John reached down carefully and plucked at both fasteners simultaneously. The plate release to reveal a small false bottom compartment. John handed the plate to Preacher as he examined the contents. In a delicate pile of wood shavings, was an elongated and round wooden box.

John reached down and gently picked up the box in his hands. Made of thin cedar wood slats, it was naturally aromatic and resistant to the elements. The surface of the wood had small intricate symbols carved into it. A single brass hasp with a small hook held the hinged lid tightly closed.

Silently, Preacher took a step closer and looked around John's shoulder. John glanced at Bob and then back at the small box. Using his thumb, John slid the hook from the hasp. Slowly, John opened the hinged lid. "What the..." John muttered at the sight... Inside the box, a small glass vial housed in a tight bed of pulled cotton. Carefully, John plucked the glass cylinder from its container. He held it up to the light. It was full of a deep red fluid. "Blood." John immediately thought. The mouth of the tube, sealed with a stout cork, then dipped into a heavy coat of red wax to ensure it was well sealed and not easily opened. The letter "D" pressed and formed into the wax.

"Is that what I think it is John," Preacher asked, looking at John with slight concern. "I believe so, Preacher," John answered. "But who's blood is it, and what is it for, I don't know," John added. "Maybe Kate can help us figure that out," John said, placing the vial back into the small box. "Of course." Preacher said, nodding in agreement.

"Can I take these," John asked to verify. "Of course, Brother, take it!" Bob said. "Wonderful!" John said, placing the box in a deep pocket in his coat and carefully wrapping the ancient book back into the fabric. "Ok, Preacher, we will be in touch," John said, tucking the book safely under his arm. "I'm at the hotel if you need me," he added. "Right, right," Preacher muttered, "Godspeed, John," he said, patting John on the back.

"Let's ride bud," John said as Zed excitedly rose to his paws. With that, John and Zed turned, walked out the door and down the hall toward the exit as Preacher followed...

The Dating Game

Chapter Five

I t was Friday, early evening in Dyer. Giving it a shake, John pulled the fuel nozzle from the tank and placed it back onto the pump. He screwed the gas cap back on and turned, walking toward the station to pay on the gas. The air was crisp with a slight breeze and not a cloud in the sky. The stars were beginning to brighten, and John knew it was going to be a cold but dry winter night in Dyer.

John reached the door as another patron was coming out. The man held the door for John. "Merry Christmas," the man said as John walked past. "Merry Christmas to you," John returned with a smile. John was excited about his date with Kate and almost forgot that the holiday was but just a few days away.

"Eighteen on five," John said to the man at the counter, reaching for his money clip. "Anything else for you tonight?" the attendant asked, taking the crisp twenty from John's grasp. On an impulse, John reached over to a small bucket of fresh single stem cut flowers by the register. "Yeah, I'll take one of these too," John said, pulling a white bloomed carnation from the chilled water. "Thank you, and please come again. Have a Merry Christmas," the attendant said, returning his change with a smile. "You too," John said, palming his coins and turning for the door. John smiled at another employee who was restocking the Big Gulp foam cups in the dispenser. As John made his way out the door, Christmas bells jingled in the doorway. Moments later, John was in the fueled-up jeep and on his way to pick up Kate.

John pulled the jeep into the parking space and turned off the engine. As he opened the door, the dome light illuminated, and John took a quick glance in the mirror to check how he looked. John grunted as he pulled his eye patch off and placed it in the console. It was already dark, and he didn't need it. John exited the jeep, closed the door, and attempted to shake his nervousness as he walked up the sidewalk to Kate's building.

There was a knock at the door. "Come on in, it's open." John opened the door and walked in. He turned and quietly closed the door. "John, is that you?" Kate asked from down the short hall. "It is," John answered, taking a deep breath. He glanced around and noticed all of the unopened boxes, misplaced knick-knacks, and scattered furniture still in disarray from his last visit.

"Sorry for the mess, I still haven't had much time to unpack," Kate said. "It's been really busy at work." John began to calm, seeing that Kate was in the middle of a mess as well. "Don't apologize, I understand." John could see Kate's shadow on the wall from where he stood scrambling to get ready for their date. "I would have been ready sooner, but I couldn't find my clothes." "That's not such a bad thing..." John whispered playfully to himself with a smile. "What was that?" Kate said as suddenly she appeared from the hallway.

John's mouth dropped. There, stood Kate. In a short, body-hugging black dress. Her blond hair was down, slightly curled. Her face glowed, with just a touch of make-up and a crimson shade of lipstick. She smiled at John. "Well, are you ready?"

John took an audible gulp. "Wow! I mean, yeah." It was the first time John had ever seen Kate in something other than nursing scrubs. "Well, let's go," Kate said as she picked up her coat in her arms and pulled at the spaghetti-strap of her small matching purse from the back of the chair. "Wait!" John motioned for Kate to stop as she attempted to walk to the door. "What is it?" Kate asked, stopping in front of John.

John stepped square to Kate and, with a fluid motion, -like a well-trained magician- produced the fresh white carnation seemingly out of thin air. Kate smiled with surprise as John gently placed the flower in her hair just above her left ear. "There, perfect. Now we can go," John said with a smile, lifting the coat from Kate's forearm. He opened the coat to her, and she twirled to allow John to fit her with the garment. "Wow, I'm impressed," Kate said as she turned to face John with a smile. "My lady," John said, smiling back, opening the door for Kate. She softly touched John on the arm as she made her way through the door and out into the hall. John followed behind, closing the door. Kate snuggled lightly against John as she locked the door. John finally began to calm as the sweet scent of Kate's perfume reached his nose. "Shall we?" John said, smiling, pointing down the hall with an open hand. With that, they were on their way...

John pulled the door opened, and Kate walked in from the cold, followed by John. The two stopped at a podium just inside the door. Within moments a well-dressed man greeted them. "Welcome to Budapest Night Restaurant. Just the two of you tonight?" the man asked. "Yes, sir," John said. "Very good, may I take your coats?" the man asked as he came around to the front of the podium. "Thank you," Kate said, turning to the man as he helped remove her coat. John also removed his jacket and handed it to the gentleman. Another employee came to take the coats from the man and hang them neatly on hangers near the entrance.

"Please, follow me," the man said as he made his way into the dining room. Kate and John followed. The moderately busy restaurant had just opened in town and boasted the finest Hungarian cuisine. The decor was loud, yet settle, as authentic Hungarian folk music played softly in the background.

The man led the two to a small bistro-style table. "Is this suitable?" the man asked, pulling the chair for Kate. "Yes, it is," John said as Kate took a seat. John pulled his chair out and also sat. "My name is Albert, and I will be your server for tonight. May

I interest you in a wine list?" the man asked. "Actually, how about a bottle of your finest Tokaji?" John said. "Ahhh, yes, excellent, sir! May I also interest you in our special for this evening," the man said. "We have our goulash served with langos." "That sounds perfect to me. I'll take it," Kate said without hesitation. "Yes, that sounds great to me as well," John added. "Very good," the waiter replied as he poured two glasses of ice water and collected the menus from the table. The waiter made his way to the kitchen to prepare their meals.

"So Kate, you didn't stay in your Aunt's house?" John asked. "Well, no. It became a big mess," Kate answered. "How so?" John asked, taking a sip of his water. "Well, some of my relatives, on my Aunt's side, when they heard Auntie had past, well, they came running. It turns out, she didn't have a will, and everyone started fighting over everything." "Oh no," John sighed, shaking his head as Kate continued. "Yeah, so long story short, they all decided to sell everything and split the money." "I'm sorry, Kate," John said sympathetically. "Oh, that's ok." Kate began to giggle. "Turns out, Auntie was way behind on her taxes, and the house was in foreclosure. So they lost the house and only got a fraction of what they thought they were going to get after they sold all of her belongings in an auction. They could have probably had a yard sale and made more money." Kate continued to laugh as John also laughed at their misfortune. "I'm sorry, Kate. You didn't get anything out of it?" John asked. Kate stopped laughing and paused. "I got her favorite teacup," she said quietly as she smiled at John, trying to hold back tears. John could see the sadness in her eyes. "It's ok, Kate." John reached across the table and held out his open hand. Kate smiled and reached back and held John's hand as a tear rolled down her cheek. John smiled back.

"Your wine, sir," the waiter said as he rolled a cart to the table with a chilled bottle and two wine glasses. Within a few moments, the waiter popped the cork and poured the bubbly. "Enjoy. Your meal will be ready shortly," the waiter said as Kate and John began to enjoy the wine. "That is good," John said, taking a sip. "Yes, it is," Kate added. "The bubbles tickle my nose." John and Kate laughed.

"So, what did Preacher find?" Kate asked, taking another sip of her Tokaji. "Well, we need your help, Kate," John said. "Sure, what can I do?" Kate responded immediately. "Do you, or do you know anyone who does lab work on blood at the hospital?" John asked. "Yeah, of course. Why?" Kate asked, intrigued. "Preacher found an old locked chest at the church. And the key that Zed found, opened it," John said. "Wow, really? So what was in it?" Kate asked. "A sealed vial of what appears to be, blood. Among a few other things," John replied, taking a sip of wine. "And you want to test the blood?" Kate asked. "Yes. The vial is sealed with a cork and then sealed again with a thick coating of wax. Then it was hidden in a compartment in a chest, and the chest itself was hidden. So I want to find out what is so special about this blood," John added. "Wow." Kate thought as John did.

The waiter suddenly appeared with a tray. Carefully, he placed a bowl of steaming hot goulash in front of Kate and then set a bowl of the same in front of John. It smelled delicious. The waiter then placed a basket of fresh langos to the center of the table. "Anything else I can get for you?" the waiter asked. "No, I think we are good, thank you," John answered. "Very good. Enjoy your meal." The man turned with the empty tray and meandered around the tables and back to the kitchen.

"Oh my God, this is divine," Kate said as she tasted a spoonful of the stew. John smiled at the sight of Kate's happiness. "Are you enjoying yourself, Kate?" John asked. Kate looked up at John and smiled. "I am. I needed this." "Me too, Kate, me too," John added as he dipped a piece of langos in his bowl of goulash...

Meanwhile, across town, at the Greater Dyer Church...

Preacher Bob stood at the podium, humming a Christmas tune as he highlighted the topics he would discuss at Sunday's sermon. "And a glorious lesson this will be," Preacher said to himself, proud of his work.

He closed his bible and shuffled his notes square on the podium. He turned and walked down the hall to his office. Moments later, he emerged dressed in his coat and carrying his briefcase. He turned and pulled the door closed. He placed the case to his side on the floor as he locked the door. Preacher picked up his case and juggled his keys into his pocket with his free hand.

He began to whistle a hymn as he walked toward the exit doors. Preacher smiled as he was amazed at the acoustics of the new building. "My, my, my, God is great," he whispered and smiled at his new church empire. He stopped near a wall and flipped a series of switches as the building's lights turned off.

Preacher walked out into the brisk cold of the evening and closed the entrance door. With the turn of a key, he locked the door and turned to be on his way. He began to whistle once again, briefcase in hand, as he walked toward his car. There was not a cloud in the sky, the moonlight was bright on the landscape, and the stars were gleaming.

Preacher came to the edge of the parking lot from the sidewalk and lifted his keys. With the press of a button on the remote, the headlights illuminated, and doors unlocked on his new Lincoln Mark VII. He walked to the driver's side and opened the door. He bent down and slid his briefcase to the backseat floorboard. As he stood up and took a step forward to get into the car, he did not notice a towering dark figure that seemed to materialize suddenly just a few paces from the back of the vehicle. The figure stood motionless as Preacher got in, pulled the door shut, put the key in the ignition, and started the car.

Preacher popped in a cassette of his favorite holiday music. The uplifting tune began to play through the high-fidelity stereo system as Preacher checked his mirrors and shifted the car into reverse. The car backed up and unexpectedly came to a sudden stop. It was enough to jolt Preacher in the seat.

"What in God's glory?" Preacher proclaimed, pressing the brake and putting the car into park. He glanced in the rearview mirrors and saw nothing. Still bewildered, Preacher opened the car door and stepped out. Both feet planted, he pulled himself from the car and stood up and turned to face the rear of the running vehicle. His eyes widened with sudden terror.

An ominous figure stood, with familiar glowing yellow eyes, staring down Preacher. It was over six feet tall and had a monstrous frame of a body. With a gasp, Preacher turned and scrambled back into the car as quickly as he could, pulling the door closed and locking it.

"My God, my God, my God!" Preacher screamed as he put the car into drive and floored it. At the same time, the figure reached down and grabbed under each side of the rear bumper. With inhuman strength, the fiend lifted the rear of the car from the pavement. The rear tires spun in midair, as the engine raced and Preacher began to panic. The creature raised the back of the vehicle from the ground higher and higher. Within a few moments, the car began to tilt sideways in the air.

"No, no, no, no!" Preacher screamed in horror and by habit, pressed the brake pedal, hoping the nightmare would just "stop." With the car's tires locked, it only made things worse, as the fiend's strength and leverage made it easy to turn the car on its side then flip it violently onto its roof. The car's momentum scraped it across the pavement in a shower of sparks. Preacher's limp body fell out of the seat to the roof as he became disorientated by the music, flickering interior lights, and sounds of twisting steel, plastic, and breaking glass. The running engine began to spit and sputter and then died out. Suddenly, the car started to spin on its roof faster and faster, making it almost impossible for Preacher to gain his bearings.

"In the name of all that is holy, I command you in God's name to STOP!" Preacher mustered his courage yelling out in all directions closing his eyes. The spinning of the vehicle slowed, and then stopped. The only sound was distorted music crackling through the rattling speakers. Preacher opened his eyes and quickly pressed the power off to the car stereo. He could hear his heart pounding in fear as he glanced around, looking for his attacker. Preacher nervously reached for the glove box and, with trembling hands, was able to open it. His shaking hands fumbled through the scattered contents and found a crucifix he kept in the vehicle.

He kissed the wooden and pewter cross and held it tight as he looked around the outside of the overturned car. He saw nothing. He heard nothing. It was quiet...

The interior lights and headlights flashed as the car alarm chirped, and the doors unlocked. Preacher gasped. A moment later, as if a bomb went off, the driver's door launched open with great force and exploded off the hinges. Preacher watched as the door twirled through the air and skipped across the parking lot, sparks scraping behind. Try as he might, Preacher could see no one.

Suddenly, from out of nowhere, a massive forearm came into the overturned car, and a powerful clawed palm grasped firmly around Preacher's throat. With great strength, Preacher violently upheaved through the open driver's door and out into the open air.

He found himself clamped by the neck and off the ground. A glowing-eyed vampire bearing gritting fangs held him at arm's-length. Preacher, still holding the crucifix in his grasp, swung his arm up and held the cross to the beast. With a slight sneer, the vampire reached up and placed his free clawed-hand directly onto the cross with no fear.

"Wealth has made your faith weak, preacher," the beast growled, crushing the crucifix like a tin can and pulling it from Preacher's grasp.

The vampire dropped the twisted relic to the ground as Preacher used both hands to pound on the creature's arm with no effect. The vampire smiled at Preacher's feeble attempt. "I am here to claim what is mine, preacher. Where is the chest and all that it contains?"

Preacher struggled to speak, "I don't have.. I don't have it!"

"Well, then we have a problem," the vampire replied. With great strength, Preacher's limp body suddenly catapulted through the air and slammed into the cold pavement, rolling and twisting several times.

Preacher laid in a heap with the wind knocked out of him. He could taste the blood in his mouth. He tried to sit up as the vampire walked toward him slowly. "If you do not possess the chest, then where shall I find it?" The creature asked, standing at Preacher's feet, looking down upon him.

Trying to catch his short breath, Preacher tried to speak. "I.. Don't.. Know.." The words were labored and short. The vampire reached down and again, grasped Preacher around the throat. He lifted him slowly from the pavement as Preacher moaned in pain. "You will learn that if I ask, then you will answer," the beast growled, pulling Preacher within inches of his foul breath and sinister glowing eyes. Preacher's head looked like a small grapefruit in the creature's enormous palm.

Preacher's eyes widened in terror as the master vampire locked his gaze with his. Preacher began to hear voices as he became locked in a powerful hypnotic trance. Words were spoken, and pictures flashed through Preacher's mind as the vampire probed his thoughts for answers.

"Bishop," the creature whispered, pulling it from Preacher's deep thoughts. The vampire spit at the sound of the name. He had his answer. The fiend pulled out of Preacher's mind as he still held his neck tight in his grip. "Now, preacher man, you will give Bishop a message," the creature whispered, reaching up with his free claw to Preacher's face.

Preacher began to scream in pain as the monster smiled, slicing Preacher's forehead with his sharp vampire nails. The beast wickedly laughed as screams of agony carried through the crisp night air...

Nightcap

Chapter Six

I t was just about 10:30 p.m. as John pulled the jeep into Kate's apartment complex parking lot. Clouds now made their way into Dyer and covered the star-lit sky as light snowflakes began to fall gracefully.

"John, I had a wonderful time tonight," Kate said, as John shifted into park. John looked over at Kate and smiled. "So did I." "Come in for a quick nightcap?" Kate asked as she clasped her hand over John's wrist softly, looking into his eyes with a pleasant smile. "Of course," John answered quickly.

John exited the vehicle, closed the door, and walked around to the passenger side. He opened the door, and Kate unexpectedly jumped out as John caught her in his arms and lowered her softly to the ground. They both giggled and held each other tight for a moment, enjoying each other's company. "Come on," John said quietly as he closed the jeep door, and they walked arm in arm up the sidewalk leading to Kate's building.

Moments later, the elevator door opened, and Kate emerged fumbling for her keys as John followed close behind. They both stopped in the hall, and Kate began to unlock the door. They could both hear the phone ringing from inside. "Wonder who that could be this late?" Kate said as the door opened. Flipping the switch for the lights, Kate rushed in, tossing her small purse to the table and reached for the ringing kitchen phone. John walked in behind, closing the apartment door.

"Hello," Kate said as she answered the phone. "Hey Lisa," Kate replied as she looked over at John with concern. "I was out with John. What? When?.." John's keen hearing could hear the frantic voice on the other end of the phone. "Oh my God! Ok, ok. We're on our way!" Kate hung up the phone and looked at John shockingly. "It's Preacher! Something bad happened! He's at the hospital!" "Come on, come on, let's go!" John said, opening the door and holding out his hand to Kate. Hand in hand, the two bolted out the door on their way to the hospital.

Minutes later, the doors to the emergency entrance at the Dyer Hospital slid open, as Kate and John raced to the front desk where they met Lisa, who was on desk duty.
Lisa jumped to her feet from her chair. "Kate! Hey John! I see you found her," Lisa said with a smile, winking at Kate for her good fortune and looking John up and down with a playful under-the-breath moan. "So, what happened?" Kate asked, embarrassed, trying quickly to change the subject.
"Oh, well, they found Preacher Bob a couple of hours ago, pretty tore up." Lisa turned and picked up Preacher's file from a wall holder, opened it, and continued. "They found him at the church, lying in the parking lot. His car looked like it was in a bad accident." "Accident in the parking lot?" John asked, confused as Lisa came around the desk. She prompted Kate and John to follow her as she made her way through the doors to the hospital ward. Lisa continued. "Yeah, the car was flipped over on the roof, and the driver's door was found across the parking lot, along with Preacher."
"How bad is it," John asked as the three walked down the hall. "Pretty bad. He's got a collapsed lung, fractured collarbone, broken leg, bruised larynx, a few teeth knocked out and more cuts, scrapes, and bruises, so yeah, he's pretty fucked up! Kate and John looked at each other quietly with concern as they reached Preacher's room.
"Well, here we are. He's pretty sedated and been talking some crazy shit, so just be patient with him. With this, Lisa handed

Kate the manila file folder containing Preacher's stats and began to walk back down the hall. As John walked into the room, Kate looked back as Lisa bent over, smacking her ass and playfully thrusting her hips, giving Kate a thumbs up on John. Blushing with a big smile, Kate turned and walked into the room.

Kate joined John at Preacher's bedside. Hooked up to multiple monitors, IVs, and other medical devices, Preacher was worse for wear. With a fresh cast on his leg, his arm in a sling to immobilize his broken collarbone, wearing a neck brace, and a large gauze taped in place on his forehead, he wasn't a pleasant sight. John leaned in and whispered, "Robert." Preacher's eyes fluttered open. "Hey, Preacher," Kate said with a smile reaching for his hand and giving it a soft squeeze. Preacher squeezed back. "Brother John.. Sister Kate..." Preacher tried to blink his eyes to focus better on the two. "My, my, my... What have we gotten into?" Preacher muttered softly with a weak and groggy voice.

"What happened Preacher?" John asked as he focused on the man's words. "I found the owner of the ring." John's face fell. "What?" Preacher gulped in pain. "Big... Big... Strong somebitch. And he wants his box back." "The chest," John said to verify. "Yes, he wants the blood." Preacher muttered as his eyes began to roll from the meds. "The blood, something is really special about that blood," John said, turning to Kate. "We need to find out and fast." Kate nodded in agreement. "He's coming back..." Preacher mumbled three last words then fell unconscious once again. He was out..

"Damn," John whispered as he suddenly focused on the gauze taped to Preacher's forehead. Quietly, John reached over and began to peel the tape from one corner of the dressing gently. "John, what are you doing?" Kate asked, pulling slightly on John's arm. "Hold on," John said, tapping Kate's hand softly.

John continued to pull at the dressing's edge until it was loose. "What the?" Kate whispered as John pulled the gauze to one side. Kate gasped, covering her mouth at the sight. John took a deep breath and dropped his head in disbelief.

Etched into the skin on Preacher's forehead, were the bloody letters spelling out the name, "Delgado." "John, you know what that means?" Kate asked. John nodded solemnly, "Yeah, and it's not good." Taking a moment to compose himself, John reached into his coat pocket. He pulled out a sterling silver mini goblet and placed it on a nearby bed tray. Reaching into another pocket, he retrieved a small plastic bottle. John opened the bottle and poured a small amount of the liquid into the goblet. "Is that what I think it is?" Kate asked, pulling closer to John's side. "It is," John said with a smile.

John dipped his thumb into the goblet of Holy water as he began to pray. "By this holy water and by Your Precious Blood, wash away all that is evil and unnatural. Protect us with your light and show us the way through the darkness, amen." "Amen," Kate added. Reaching over, John made the sign of the cross upon Preacher's scarred forehead.

As John and Kate stood and watched, the bloody letters on Preacher's forehead suddenly began to fade. The surface bruises and scratches also started to disappear or heal. Any wounds directly caused by the vampire's touch were no longer, although the broken bones and other injuries caused by trauma were still present and needed time to heal.

"We need to test that blood now," John said to Kate as he pulled the rest of the dressing from Preacher's forehead and threw it in the trash. "I can get us access to the lab," Kate said, ready to help. "I want to test it on human blood and vampire blood," John said, placing the Holy water and silver goblet back into his pocket. "Wait, vampire blood?" Kate asked. "So, where are we going to get vampire blood?"

John stopped and smiled at Kate. "No, not "we." Zed, and I will get the vampire blood." "Oh no, John, I'm coming with you and Zed," Kate demanded. John sighed, "It's too dangerous, Kate." "John, look around, this danger is everywhere. I was in the middle of it with you, remember? Look, the only way to be safe is to understand it, deal with it, and fight it. And you are the best person I know to show me how to do all those things."

John thought for a moment, knowing that Kate was right, but

he knew his feelings for her were starting to get in the way. "Ok, Kate. Ok." Reluctantly, John agreed with a soft nod. Kate smiled. "Ok, then. So what do we do first?" John thought for a moment.. "We need a couple of blood collection kits." "I'm on it," Kate said, heading for the door. "Kate," John called out. "Yes," she answered, stopping at the door. John eyed her up and down in her little black dress and pumps. "That's not really the proper vampire hunting attire," John said, turning slightly red in the face. Kate smiled, "I think I have something more appropriate in my locker. I'll be back."

A few minutes later, Kate returned to Preacher's room, where John was waiting. "Better?" she asked, modeling a tight pair of jeans, a blue button-down shirt, and black flats. She still had the carnation in her hair. "What about the flower?" John asked with a smile. Kate smiled, sauntering toward John. "Well, technically, we are still on our date, so the flower stays." With a last check on Preacher, Kate and John collected their belongings and headed out the door.
"We'll stop and pick up Zed," John said as he opened the jeep door for Kate. She climbed into the seat as John closed the door and made his way around to the driver's side. He jumped in and turned over the engine. He turned on the headlights and clicked the wipers to clear the windshield of the light coating of snow. John backed the jeep from the parking spot, shifted into drive, and drove off into the cold, snowy night...

John pulled the jeep off the highway into the hotel's parking lot. He put it into park and left the engine running. "I'll be just a minute," John said to Kate as he opened the jeep door. John closed the door and walked toward his hotel room. From inside, the light and TV were on, and a shadow shifted quickly across the room.
Zed knew the sound of the running jeep. Kate watched out the windshield with a smile. Zed peaking from under the pulled curtains and out the window, watched excitedly as John

reached the hotel room door. Zed's head suddenly disappeared from sight as John opened the door.

"Come on, bud. You're on the clock," John said, ruffling Zed's giant head. With that, Zed let out a sharp bark and raced toward the running jeep as John closed and locked the room door. John trotted back to the vehicle, opened the driver's door, and Zed leapt up and in, to greet Kate with a warm lick to the face. "Hey buddy, yeah, good to see you too," Kate laughed, rubbing all over Zed's floppy head.

"Ok, bud, backseat," John said, making sure his pack was on the back seat floorboard. Zed jumped to the back as John pulled himself into the driver's seat. John slammed the door and looked at Kate. "Well, ready to do some vampire hunting?" Kate looked at John with a smile. "You know how ridiculous that would sound coming from someone else?" Both John and Kate giggled, as John put the jeep in drive and peeled the tires as they pulled out of the lot.

"So, where are we going exactly?" Kate asked, bundling her coat around herself. "Have you ever heard of the little town of Kelton?" John asked, turning the volume down on the radio. "Yeah, it's all but abandoned," Kate replied. "That's exactly what we're looking for. It's about 75-80 miles from here, right?" John asked. "Yeah, just keep on the highway. I think it runs right through it.. Or what's left of it anyway." Kate answered.

"So who is this "Delgado" anyways?" Kate asked, looking to John. No answer... "John," Kate whispered, touching his arm gently. John let out a deep sigh. "Victor Delgado. A very dangerous entity. Wherever he goes, bad things happen." John stretched his neck. "He is a vampire?" Kate asked, focusing on John over the radio. John nodded. "Yes, not only a vampire, but a true Blood Lord. Very powerful, smart, and dangerous. And he came after Preacher. Somehow, Victor knew that Preacher had the chest. But how?" John thought for a moment.

"Well, who knew that Preacher had the chest?" Kate answered John's question with another question. "Of course," John began to realize. "The construction workers that found the chest, before they went and got Preacher. The board members of the Dyer Historical Society. It had to be a human familiar." John smacked the steering wheel. "That's gotta be it! But who was it?" John said in bewilderment. Kate looked at John, confused. "So, what is a familiar?" John smiled and looked at Kate. "Well, "familiars" are humans that have devoted themselves to a vampire and pledged themselves to a house or specific vampire leader." John reached over and turned the stereo down and continued... "They're given perks- riches, lavish lifestyles, protection, one of which if they prove themselves worthy, their "master" would turn them, and they would be gifted immortality." "Wow," Kate whispered at the thought.

"Hey," John glared over at Kate. "What?" Kate asked, suddenly feeling scolded. "I just noticed something." "What?" Kate asked quickly. "Since I've seen you, I haven't seen you smoke." "Oh," Kate said, relieved with a smile. "I quit a while back." "Really?" John said with a smirk. "Yes, I remember you said you quit, and I thought, well, if you could quit, so could I. And I did. It was a bad habit, anyway." Kate smiled at her accomplishment. "Good for you, Kate. Good for you!" John smiled, reached over, and squeezed her knee softly. Kate touched the top of John's hand as soon, both were holding hands.

"Well, it'll be a little bit before we get there. Why don't you try and get some sleep? Might be a long night." John said as he turned the heat up a tad. "Ok," Kate said, as she pulled the white carnation from her hair as not to crush it. She laid the flower on the warm dash of the jeep and leaned over and snuggled into John's side. Kate was calm and felt warm and safe with John and Zed. John smiled as he reached over and turned the music back up slightly as the radio played REO Speedwagon's, "Keep On Loving You."

Kelton

Chapter "Lucky" Seven

I t was about two hours later. The drive was slow going out of Dyer, due to a few heavy snowfall bands, which made visibility nearly impossible. The further John, Kate, and Zed drove toward Kelton, it cleared up, and the road conditions became better. Luck appeared to be on their side, as the jeep was just outside the village limits. The temperature was slightly warmer, still cold, though no snow at all, either falling or on the ground.

"Kate, wakey, wakey, beautiful," John whispered in Kate's ear. Kate's eyes fluttered open, and she sat up, peering through the windows, trying to gain her bearings. "We're here?" she asked, plucking her carnation from the dash and setting it back into her hair above her left ear. "Almost. We'll be coming into the village limits in a few." John answered, flicking the brights beginning to study the surroundings.

"What's that noise?" Kate asked, hearing something like a growl or a sneer over the radio. John smiled. "That's Zed snoring in the back." Kate began to laugh, looking to the back seat. "Yeah, he's been out for a while too," John said, looking in the rearview mirror at the four paws sticking in the air.

"Watch this," John whispered to Kate as she continued to laugh at the intense snoring. "Zed," John said. The snoring continued. "Zed," John said louder and firmly. Nothing.. "Zed!" John shouted one more time. Another snore. Kate was in tears laughing. John held up his finger to Kate to wait. "Does someone want... A cookie," John said quietly. Suddenly the back seat thrashed. In a split second, Zed's large head was in the front of the jeep between Kate and John with droopy twitching eyes, a bent ear, and hanging slobber. Kate lost it with intense laughter as John reached into his front pocket to retrieve a "cookie" for Zed. "Hey, buddy! Good to see you could join us." John said as he poked the cookie into Zed's open jaw.

"Ok, we have to get ready," John said as his tone became more serious. "Ok," Kate said. "Now, if we do find a vampire out here, it might be a little different," John said to Kate. "Different how?" Kate asked, sounding concerned. "Well, it's very isolated out here, so we may encounter what I call "feral" vampires." Kate thought for a moment. "Feral? You mean like a feral cat or something?" "Yeah, kind of. They may be different, wilder than usual. They may not have a "master" or a leader and just seem like they're lost or crazy. And they'll probably be afraid of us and run." John said, slowing the jeep down. "Really? Wow." Kate replied. "Yeah, they may have been turned, and don't realize what happened, so they run and isolate themselves and survive not knowing what to do. So with no intelligent interactions, leadership, or stimulation, they get a little crazy. And with no people around, they feed on anything they can find. Animals, dirt, bugs, each other. And they may be extra ugly in appearance." John added. "Extra ugly?" Kate asked perplexed. "Yeah, like crooked fangs, crossed eyes, harelips. Kinda like "hick" vampires," John said. "John," Kate said, covering her mouth, trying not to laugh, feeling a little offended by John's description. "Well, I'm just saying," John added with a smile.

An approaching faded and rusting sign came into the view of the headlights. It read, "Kelton village limits. Pop. 157." John turned off the headlights and just illuminated the parking lamps of the jeep. The moon was out and bright enough that it lit the surrounding landscape with an eerie glow.

The entire village was dark, as it was abandoned, or so it seemed at first. "Zed, stand fast. Watch em." John said as Zed immediately perked up and stood straight, peering out the windshield with his keen eyesight.

"So, what are we looking for exactly?" Kate asked as she also looked out into the darkness. "You'll know when we see it," John said as he once again downshifted and slowed the jeep to a steady roll. Old abandoned and condemned houses stood just off the road to either side. Overgrown, dead shrubs and tall grass cast creepy shadows on the blighted landscape in the moonlight.

Suddenly, John locked up the brakes, and Kate let out a short scream as a figure ran across the front of the jeep. Zed barked as his eyes followed the fleeing character. "Ok, here we go. Ready?" John asked Kate as he pulled the vehicle off the road and put it into park. "Yep," Kate replied nervously, grabbing her bag of blood testing kits and a silver crucifix from the floorboard.

"Zed, corral," John commanded as he opened the driver's door and planted his feet to the ground. With a short bark, Zed leapt from the jeep and hit the ground running. Within seconds he was on the heels of the figure. John pulled his bag from the back floorboard as Kate jumped out and ran around the front of the vehicle to meet him. "Come on," John said, holding his hand out to Kate. Hand in hand, John and Kate ran through the tall grass to catch up to Zed.

The fleeing creature made it to a large oak tree in the yard of an abandoned house. Looking back at Zed, the crazed man hissed and clawed his way up the tree like a wild animal. Zed stood at the trunk of the tree with his front paws extended upward on the tree. The dog barked as the man struggled to climb higher.

John and Kate stopped yards short of where Zed was, behind the side of a broken-down Ford T-bird to assess what was happening. "Ok, stay here for a minute. Let me check it out," John said to Kate. She nervously nodded in agreement. With that, John jumped from behind the car and was at Zed's side within a few moments. "What you got, bud?" John said as he looked up into the tree. Zed's tail wagged with excitement as he looked upward, keeping his eyes on the figure through the bare branches.

It was what John expected. A rogue vampire. Barefoot, in tattered jeans and a ripped "Ratt" concert t-shirt. The vampire hissed and growled as its glowing eyes darted around frantically to find a means of escape.

Nearby, Kate quietly walked to the back of the car to watch John and Zed try to capture the creature. Without warning, the trunk lid burst open on rusted hinges, and a frail-framed, half-naked vampire launched herself from the dark confines of the trunk and landed feet first in front of a terrified Kate.

Kate stood up in horror and looked the glowing-eyed creature eye to eye. "Kate!" John yelled, turning his attention from the creature high in the tree. Wide-eyed, Kate tried to catch her breath, looking the fiend up and down. The vampiress stood silent for a moment, tilting her head of tangled hair, seemingly shocked at Kate's beauty. The vampire wore a short, torn jean skirt with ripped fish-net stocking. She had no shirt; her bare breasts were slightly lopsided and one, with a pierced nipple. She had an incomplete tattoo of a butterfly on her arm and one of a small black heart on her cheek. There were numerous fang marks on her breast and neck, with trickles of dried blood. One side of her jaw was exposed entirely as if her flesh was ripped from her face.

The vampiress stood with searing, glowing eyes and smiled at Kate as the exposed tendons in her jaw stretched to reveal jagged fangs. Gathering herself, Kate pulled her arm up and held the cross to the monster. The creature hissed, but stood her ground. "Believe Kate, have faith, Kate," John said calmly, as he stopped a few yards from where the standoff was taking place. Zed continued to hold the creature in the tree, ready to help Kate on command.

Kate's face changed as she gained confidence. "Back," Kate commanded as the creature began to cower from the cross. "I said back, bitch!" Kate yelled as she took a bold step toward the vampiress pressing the crucifix to the fiend's grotesque face. A sudden, inhuman screech came from the creature. It backed, turned, and bolted in a panic across the yard toward the safety of an abandoned house.

"Zed, get her," John commanded as he also ran, trying to cut her path off to the house. Zed took off from his spot at the tree and raced to intercept the vampiress. Kate took a breath at what she had just done. She watched as the creature sped by John and then just barely got by Zed to make her way inside the open door of the dark house. But Zed was on her heels.

"Kate, come on," John said, stopping on the porch of the house, as Zed's barks and the vampire's screeches and growls could be heard from inside.

Kate gathered herself and felt her adrenaline rush as she ran to join John.

John pulled a flashlight from his ready bag and gave it to Kate. "Here. Be very careful. Come on," John said as he took a step into the dark doorway. His keen night vision kicked in, and he saw Zed had the vampire blocked into an adjacent corner. Kate followed John just inside the door and lit the flashlight. The vampiress hissed as Kate shined the bright light into the creature's wicked eyes.

"Zed, keep her pegged," John commanded. The K9 stood silent and still, ready to attack if the vampire moved. "Kate, get a blood kit," John said as he moved carefully on the other side of Zed to box in the creature. Kate placed the flashlight under her arm and unzipped her handbag to retrieve a kit.

There was a sudden rustle from a rotting sofa in the room just off to Kate's right. Kate looked up as a feral cat darted out from under the couch and straight for the open door, exactly where Kate was standing. Kate screamed in terror as the wild cat hissed and ran through her legs and out the door. John and Zed turned their attention to Kate. "Fucking cats! I hate cats!" Kate yelled out as she stomped up and down.

With the distraction, it was just enough to allow the cornered vampire to attempt an escape. The creature pulled at a heavy bookcase that was against the wall. The large shelving unit began to fall toward Zed. Dusty books started to thump to the floor. "Zed, back!" John screamed as he saw what was happening out of the corner of his eye. Zed turned back to see the shelf tipping.

Zed twirled his body and kicked his powerful hind legs and cleared the shelf at the last second as the large case crashed to the floor. A cloud of dense dust filled the room. At that moment, the vampire leapt over the fallen case and bolted toward a decaying staircase that led upstairs.

"Shit," John muttered as he quickly meandered around the room of scattered furniture, trying to cut off the fleeing creature. As the vampire reached the bottom of the stairs, John met the beast with a raised silver crucifix. The vampiress screeched and raised her arm to shield her eyes from the sight of the cross. Kate regained herself and had the flashlight beam back on John and the cowering creature. "Ok, slow it down, easy. Kate got the kit?" John asked, stepping closer to the vampire. "Yep," Kate answered. "Ok, come over, slowly." John motioned to Kate. Zed paced at Kate's side as the two carefully made their way to John and the pinned creature.

The vampire hissed and suddenly took a soft pace back onto the first step. Then took another pace back onto the next step. There was a pop and a loud creak. John turned and watched as the creature backed up another step on the staircase. Then another loud creak. "Shit," John whispered as he knew what was about to happen. "Stop!" John commanded the creature. A growl came from the vampiress as she took another careful step up the rickety staircase. Then another. Then another. And another pop and squeak came from the deteriorating flight of steps.

As the creature reached the center of the staircase, a series of creaks, groans, snaps, and pops echoed through the empty house. "No, no, no!" John screamed as suddenly a large portion of the staircase gave way, and the vampiress screeched as she dropped into the basement.

Kate and Zed stood at John's side. Kate shined the flashlight down into the fallen floor. As the dust settled, the beam of light fell onto the mangled body of the vampire. There she was, semi-buried in a pile of wooden debris, her body contorted in an unnatural position. The creature's face in a grotesque look of pain as a large splintered piece of lumber pierced through her chest. With a scream of agony, the vampiress burst into a brilliant ball of blue, yellow, and purple flames. Within moments, she was gone...

"Well, that worked well," John said as Kate coughed from the dust, and Zed sneezed. "John," Kate yelled, looking out the nearby broken window. John turned and saw the vampire that Zed had chased up a tree, now on the ground and running off on all fours, like an animal, into the darkness. "Can't we catch him?" Kate asked in excitement. "No, he's long gone," John answered, disappointed. "I don't remember these ferals being this hard to catch," he added. "Maybe we're slipping bud," John said to Zed, rubbing the top of the dog's head with a smile.

John walked just outside the open door, as Kate and Zed joined him quietly on the porch. "So now what?" Kate asked, looking to John. Taking a deep breath, John scanned the moonlit landscape. His keen eyesight suddenly caught something off in the distance. "Wait, of course. That's where we'll find one," John whispered with a smile. "Come on, let's go," John said as he led the way back to the jeep.

After a short drive, John pulled off the road and killed the engine. "Ok, were here," John said with a smile. Kate looked out the window. "Really, John?" Kate opened the door and stepped out. "Seriously?" Kate asked as John and Zed met her at the front of the jeep.

"Well, why not?" John asked with a smile, looking over the short rusted iron gate that surrounded the old Kelton cemetery. "So, do we just look for open or fresh dug graves?" Kate asked, smirking back at John. "Not exactly," John answered. "Come on." John picked up his bag of tricks, and Kate shouldered her small satchel of kits and, along with Zed, off the three went.

Quietly, the three followed the winding footpath that meandered between the numerous old headstones, monuments, statues, and tangled trees and shrubs, neglected for years. In the distance, John saw what he was looking for.

"There it is," John said quietly, feeling better about their odds of finally getting some vampire blood. Kate looked up and saw where John was heading. As the three approached, a massive structure began to rise from the dark landscape—a large family crypt, belonging to one of the first families that settled in the small town. Zed put his snout to the cold ground, as he was on to something. "What is it bud?" John whispered, as Zed followed the scent to the back of the solid stone crypt. John and Kate followed. Reaching the backside of the vault, Zed pulled at the semi-thawed ground with his paws. "Kate," John said, pointing to the earth under Zed's digging. Kate walked up next to John and hit the ground with the flashlight. Zed pulled his powerful paw back one more time as suddenly his claw caught an edge. Kate screamed in horror, as a shallow, buried skull suddenly pulled to the surface and turned to face her with a gaping jaw. "It's a good sign," John whispered. "A good sign?" Kate asked, stuttering, still trying to shake it off. "Yeah, it's probably a body that use to be in one of the crypt coffins. Something emptied the coffin so it could be used." John said with a calming smile.

"Come on," John whispered as he made his way along the edge of the structure. Zed and Kate followed carefully. As the three came to the front of the small building, there was a slight stench of death that John knew well. "Oh my God, what is that?" Kate asked, covering her nose and mouth from the foul smell. "That, my dear, is something you never get used to. Here, try this." John reached into his pocket and pulled out a small bottle. Opening the cap, he put two tiny drops on his fingers and rubbed them together. John turned to Kate and gently pulled her close.

John smiled at Kate. "God, I pray that you anoint this oil in Your heavenly name. Amen." John smeared his fingers just above Kate's top lip and under her nose. "Better?" John asked. "Wow, yeah, what is that?" Kate asked, breathing in the pleasant yet strong scent. "Cedar oil," John replied.

"Well, let's see what we've got here," John said, turning back to the crypt's entrance. Dropping his pack to the ground from his shoulder, Kate and Zed came to John's side with the flashlight.

They stood on a cracked and sunk-in series of slate tiles, badly weathered and loose from time. In front of them, a towering double iron gate. It was rust-pitted and unhinged on one corner from the stone frame of the entrance. A large chain wrapped through the center bars and secured it with a heavy padlock.

John reached up, grasped the lock in his hand, and gave it a stout pull. As he thought, the lock popped open with little effort. John could see that the lock was worked recently and often. "Another good sign," John thought as he uncoiled the heavy wrapped chain from the gate. Quietly, John placed the chain in a piled heap on the ground. He pulled one side of the gate open, and it fought hard to remain closed. As he pulled the other iron gate panel, the bolts in the loose hinge snapped and popped though it opened easier than the opposite side.

Just inside the gate was a closed, rusted-pitted, iron door. It was latched shut, although the padlock to keep it secured was gone. John pulled on the mechanism, and it released the door from the frame. He grabbed the iron handle and pulled on it slowly. A low moan reverberated through the quiet air as the heavy door swung open on the rusted and loose hinges.

A musty scent of a smell reached John's nose, along with a hint of fresh death. "Ok, we're in," John said quietly, reaching down to his pack for a few items. "Zed, stand fast and keep watch," Zed gave a low, quiet bark at John's command. "Ok, are you ready?" John asked, smiling at Kate. "No, but let's get this over with," Kate replied with a deep sigh. "It'll be ok, I promise," John said, caressing Kate's arm softly, and then reaching for her hand.

John turned and made his way into the dark tomb, taking a step down the short set of crumbling concrete steps, guiding Kate behind by the hand. Zed sat and watched patiently as the two slowly descended into the darkness.

A few moments later, John was inside at the bottom of the steps. Kate was a couple of reluctant steps behind. "You've got to be kidding me," Kate whispered, shining the flashlight just past where John stood. As Kate's eyes adjusted to the dark surroundings, she began to have second thoughts.

It was a small rectangle room, longer than it was wide. It had high walls and a vaulted ceiling. A small stone carved circular window was at its peak. The moonlight trickled in, casting the area in an eerie blue-grey glowing huge against the walls and the dark matching caskets. There were three levels of coffins, with two end to end on either side and one lining the end wall on each tier. There were a total of fifteen family member caskets.

"John, I can't," Kate whispered, overwhelmed with sudden fear. "You can, Kate," John said with encouraging words, holding out his hand to her. Taking a deep breath, Kate slowly stepped down to join John at his side. "You're safe, Kate, I'm here, and Zed's just outside. And you've seen a lot worse than this, Yes?" John asked with a smile. Kate thought for a moment, "You're right," she said with a steady nod.

"Ok, so how do we do this?" Kate asked, looking to John. "Well, we will let beauty find what we are looking for." John turned and caressed Kate's cheek in his palm with a warm touch. Kate's eyes widened with fear, "What!? John, I.. I can't," before Kate could finish her words, John reached up and plucked the white carnation from Kate's hair. Kate looked at John with surprise.

Without a word, John turned and placed the bloomed carnation on the top of the closest casket. Kate watched quietly, shining the flashlight beam onto the flower. Nothing happened. John picked up the flower and moved it to the top of the next casket lid. Again, nothing. Kate continued to follow the flower with the flashlight. John, once again, placed the carnation upon the surface of another coffin lid. As Kate and John watched, suddenly, the fresh white flower turned brown, wilted, and died falling from the stem. Kate gasped in shock.

"There we go," John said, quietly motioning for Kate to come to his side. "When I open the lid, I'll constrain it, and then I'll tell you when to do your thing. Ready?" John asked as Kate joined his side, looking to John with uncertain eyes. "You can do this, Kate," John whispered with a smile. With a deep breath and a nod from Kate, John reached down and lifted the lid to the casket.

The coffin opened to reveal a resting male vampire. The creature's glowing eyes were open and staring upward. As John and Kate stood at the edge of the casket, the vampire suddenly turned its head slowly to gaze upon the two. Kate felt unsettled as her eyes locked with the creature's silent stare. "Don't look directly at him," John said, pulling a silver crucifix from his coat as Kate pulled her look down from the creature's piercing gaze. Dressed in a tattered suit, the vampire still had a smudge of blood on its lips from a recent feed.

As the creature continued to stare down John with an unsettling leer, John pulled his arm up, wielding his silver cross to the fiend's pale face. Immediately, the vampire cowered and turned its head away from the cross with a quiet and settle hiss as it bared its fangs to John. The vampire's body remained motionless as it continued to turn its head away slowly. The sound of bones cracking began to echo through the small crypt. Its head continued to turn from the crucifix like a serpent. The creature's head turned almost entirely around, so now all that John could see was the back of its head. Kate gasped in horror at the unexpected sight. "Well, that's a new one," John quipped, also caught off guard by the creature's unorthodox action.

"Ok, Kate, now," John said as he was also shocked at the creature's 180-degree head trick. With a shaky hand, Kate handed John the flashlight and pulled out a blood kit from her small shouldered satchel. She ripped open the pouch and stepped up closer to John's side. The creature's bare forearm was visible from under a loose shirt sleeve, and Kate focused on it. She pulled the tattered cuff up and eyed a bulging vein in the vampire's arm as she let her training take over.

Within a few moments, Kate had a collection of the creature's black blood in a vile. "Get another sample to be safe," John said as he continued to press the vampire back. Quickly, Kate repeated the procedure and in moments, had another sample. To finish, Kate took a fresh, clean cotton ball, dabbed, and pressured the puncture mark of the needle. "Kate, really?" John asked with a smirk. "What?" Kate asked, looking confused at John's question. "No, really, Kate?" John asked again. "What, John?" Kate answered, becoming agitated. "Is the cotton ball really necessary? I mean, he is dead, and he's a vampire, I don't think it matters to him," John said with a slight chuckle. Thinking a moment, Kate rolled her eyes and released the pressure of the cotton swab. "Ok, I just had a blonde moment, ok," Kate said with a laugh as John handed her the flashlight back.

As Kate carefully packed the blood samples away, John lowered the crucifix and pulled a silver dagger from the back of his belt. "Asheas êon asheas êda dust êon dust, ê release vedo from vút torment, êful God'as holy nim, amen." (Translated; "Ashes to ashes and dust to dust, I release you from your torment, in God's holy name, amen.") John spoke solemnly as he raised the dagger above the creature and dropped the blade into its black heart. The vampire moaned in agony as purple, and blue flames engulfed the body. John pulled down the lid to the casket as the fire died out. He sheathed the dagger back into his belt and placed the silver cross back into his inside coat pocket.

"Alright, let's get. We've got what we need," John said. With a grateful nod from Kate, the two carefully made their way up the steps... Outside, Zed sat, still watching for any signs of danger. "Ok, Zed, we're good. Time to go bye-bye," John said as Zed rose to all four paws, gave a quick bark, and led Kate and John back through the cemetery to the jeep safely.

John turned the ignition and started the jeep. Zed settled in the back seat for a nap as Kate got comfortable at John's side for the long ride home. "Try to get some sleep, Kate. It'll take us a couple of hours to get back, and we have a long day ahead of us tomorrow," John said, as he shifted into drive and steered the jeep down the road into the cold night back toward Dyer...

Hospitatrocity

Chapter Eight

Earlier that night...

The flash of two intense glowing yellow eyes, followed by a deep growl whispering, "Preacher," suddenly caused Bob to awaken from a deep sleep unexpectedly. There was the doctor, penlight in hand, pulling each eyelid open and sweeping the beam across each slumbering eye.

"What in God's name," Preacher mumbled as he squirmed against the doctor's touch and the sudden bright light. "How are you tonight, Bob?" the doctor asked, pulling back. "Well, I believe I was better a minute ago while I was asleep. But now, thanks to you, I feel like the Devil wiped his ass with me!" Preacher gulped in pain as the doctor laughed at his remark. "Well, believe it or not, you're on the mend, Preacher. Your vitals are looking better. Very good, actually," the doctor replied, writing down Preacher's readings on his clipboard. "You should be out real soon," the doctor commented, smiling, as he hung the board at the end of the bed, turned and exited the room.

Preacher groggily sat forward slightly, then fell back as his eyes adjusted to the surroundings. He reached over, and his hand found the bed remote. With the press of a few buttons, he found the correct sequence to raise the bed slightly so he could sit up to a more comfortable position. It was strangely quiet, as all he could hear was the monitors beeping and blipping with melodic rhythm. The room, dimly lit, and the air seemed stale. He seemed to have a slight ringing in his ears.

A sudden "tap, tap" at the door, Preacher turned to see Nurse Lisa enter with a smile and a tray of food. "Dinner time Preacher Bob," she said as she pulled an adjustable rolling table over to the bed. "I'm not hungry right now, but thank you," Preacher said as Nurse Lisa adjusted the height of the table and rolled it over the bed and in front of Preacher. "You gotta eat something, baby. And afterward, we'll get you up and out for a little wheel-chair ride down to rehab and see how you do on your crutches," she said placing the tray of food on the table.

"I've had a broken leg before," Preacher said, shaking his head. "I told everyone, I know how to use crutches, but no one listens." Nurse Lisa keeled back on her heels and gave Preacher a dirty look. "Uh-umm. And I suppose you got that cut on your arm from knowing how to use crutches when you fell this morning," she replied, bobbling her head and pointing to the gauze and tape on his arm. "Ok, fine," Preacher said reluctantly with a sigh. "Eat your supper, hun. I'll be back for you," Nurse Lisa said as she pulled the cover from the warm plate of food and turned to leave with a smile.

Preacher plopped his head back into his pillow and looked up, thinking for a moment. There was a sudden flicker of the light just above his bed that caught his drifting attention. Through the ringing in his ears, Bob suddenly thought he heard a faint whisper, "Preacher..." He lifted his head and stared at the room doorway for a moment. He heard nothing else.

With a sigh, Preacher sat up and looked at the plate of food.

A scoop of mashed potatoes with a dripping of beef gravy. A thin slice of what looked to be roast beef with a scoop of white rice on the side. A bowl of steaming vegetable soup. A sealed cup of applesauce. A quarter of a cut, unpeeled banana, and a small can of juice.

"Yummy! I'm used to prime rib and lobster and now this..." Preacher mumbled as he reached for his fork. Suddenly, Preacher froze. "What the..," he whispered. His eyes focused on the rice as he thought he saw something strange. He gently poked at it with his fork. "Hmmm. I must be seeing things. Must be the drugs they're giving me," Preacher chuckled as he loaded his fork with a heap of rice. He took a bite and shook his head from the taste of the plain rice. He lifted the utensil with another helping of rice, this time dunking it into the roast beef gravy for more flavor.

As he brought the fork up, he felt something tickling the corner of his mouth. Preacher leaned his head forward and raised his other arm from the sling slightly and reached his fingers to his mouth. He plucked the piece of food with his fingers and looked at it. It moved between his fingers. It was a plump maggot. Preacher's eyes widened as he looked at the fork of food he was about to eat. It was loaded with the squirming larvae as they dropped from the fork and onto the sheets. "My God!" Preacher screamed as he pitched the utensil to the tray in terror.

Looking down in shock, his eyes focused on the bowl of soup. There were small ripples at the surface of the broth. Preacher's mouth fell open, as several small black snakes began to slither out of the liquid, over the rim of the bowl and onto the tray. At the same moment, the surface of the mashed potatoes began to crack outward, like a crusted pimple. The top of the potatoes opened to reveal a cavity full of scattering cockroaches as they crawled everywhere. Preacher closed his eyes and screamed out in horror, swatting wildly at the crawling sheets of snakes and insects.

"What is going on in here?" Nurse Lisa asked as she came running into the room from Preacher's panicked screams. Preacher opened his eyes, and there sat the tray of food, as it was- no worms, snakes, or bugs. "I...I thought I saw," Preacher stopped in mid-sentence, realizing there was nothing wrong. "I know our food isn't the best, but it ain't that bad," Nurse Lisa said, covering the plate. "Do you want any of this?" she asked, placing her hand on her hip, waiting for an answer. "No...No..." Preacher stuttered, trying to gain his composure. "And look, you pulled your dressing clean off," Nurse Lisa said, looking at the cut on

Preacher's arm. She reached down and held his arm still, looking at the bleeding scratch. "Hmmm. That's starting to look infected. I'll be back with some ointment and new dressings." She swung the table from the bed, picked up the tray of food, and walked from the room, shaking her head.

Preacher sat back, trying to calm down. The monitors were beeping wildly, in sync with his elevated heart rate. He could feel the cut on his arm stinging from being uncovered and the air hitting it. Preacher took a deep breath and began to calm down.

Preacher felt a sudden sharp twinge as he looked down at the uncovered cut. "What now," he thought as he pulled his arm closer to examine it. Slowly making a fist, it pulled his skin tight on his arm. The area around the cut was dark purple with a ring of bright red around the outside. Once again, he flexed his fist as the wound began to itch.

Unexpectedly, the cut began to throb slowly. Preacher sat up and held his arm down as he watched the cut lower and rise as if it was alive. The skin started to bubble with yellow puss as Preacher once again began to panic. He turned his head and closed his eyes. The cut suddenly popped as if it was a boil, splattering blood and puss all over his face, floor, walls, and bed sheets.

Preacher, shaking nervously, opened his eyes and looked down at his arm. "Nooooo!" Preacher screamed as he watched in complete shock and dismay. The wound in his arm was now open, leaking blood, puss, and hundreds of small black spiders scurrying in all directions. He shut his eyes from the sight and began to pray aloud.

"In the name of baby Jesus, what is going on in here?" Nurse Lisa proclaimed, walking in with a roll of gauze and tape. Preacher opened his eyes and glanced around nervously. He looked down at his arm, and it was as it was before. Just a small cut, although no puss, blood splats, or spiders.

"Nurse Lisa, I am seeing some crazy Lucifer demon Devil shit!" Preacher said excitedly, looking at the nurse with wide terror-filled eyes. Nurse Lisa planted back on her foot and stared at Preacher for a moment. "Well, Preacher, I know I ain't no Michelle Pfeiffer, but I'll try not to be so damn shocking when I come into the room! Is it because I'm black?" Nurse Lisa spouted, trying to lighten the mood with humor.

"No, no, no, Nurse Lisa, I am serious!" Preacher replied. "My Bible, I need my Bible, now!" Preacher pointed with a shaky finger to a small rectangular table against the wall under the T.V. "Ok, ok, keep your robe on Preacher," Nurse Lisa said, moving to retrieve his Bible from the top of the table.

"My Lord Preacher, what has gotten into you?" Nurse Lisa asked, handing the Good Book to his shaky grasp. "It's a pure evil that has invaded my very soul." Preacher replied, pulling the book to his lap. Nurse Lisa turned to check on his IV drip as Preacher began to flip through the pages, his trembling fingers trying to locate a particular passage...

He began to read aloud. "The Lord is my shepherd; I shall not want. He maketh me to lie down in green pastures: He leadeth me beside the still waters. He restoreth my soul: He leadeth me in the paths of righteousness for his name's sake. Yea, though I walk through the valley of the shadow of death, I will fear no evil: for thou art with me; thy..." Suddenly a drop of fresh blood appeared on the center of the right page. Preacher stopped reading and focused on the blood. The red bead cascaded gently down into the center of the book.

Preacher gulped as the center between the pages began to fill with blood. "My God in Heaven," Preacher gasped as he watched the pages of his Bible seem to bleed through. Blood began to pour and drip off the pages onto the bedding and into his lap. He could now feel a wet on his thighs and between his legs. Preacher threw his head back to his pillow and closed his eyes tight in terror. "Nurse Lisa! Can you see that? Can you see that?" Preacher cried out, now hearing the blood splattering on the floor.

"Well, my Heavens, yes, I can." Nurse Lisa answered with a sigh. "Where's it coming from? I swear it's from the Devil himself!"

Preacher screamed out still with his eyes closed. "Preacher, with all your crazy thrashing, you pulled out your catheter, and you just pissed the bed!" Preacher suddenly opened his eyes and looked down at the soaked bed sheets. "What am I going to do with you, Preacher Bob?" Nurse Lisa asked as she turned, shaking her head and leaving to get a mop, bucket, and a fresh set of sheets from the linen cart parked in the hall.

Preacher Bob looked down at his Bible and closed it slowly. With a deep breath, he pulled the book to his chest and quietly began to cry...

Blood Type OMG

Chapter Nine

T he sun broke over the barren winter landscape of Dyer. It was just a few days before Christmas, and the town was slow to wake, as the morning cold slowed the blood flow of the community. The kids were out of school, and many people were out of town on Christmas vacation. Dyer still experienced moments of old, as it continued to grow.

John stood at the window of his hotel room, sipping on a cup of fresh coffee. The weatherman on the T.V. with an optimistic tone, reporting on a good chance that Dyer would indeed see a white Christmas even though there was no snow on the ground at present. John walked to the door and opened it as Zed came racing into the room from the outside cold.

"Did you get your business done?" John asked. Zed shook his cold fur and sat at John's feet and answered with a short huffy bark. "Ok, I'll have to go and clean up your mess," John said, pulling a treat from his pocket and tossing it to Zed. With cat-like reflexes, Zed snatched it from the air and, with a few happy chomps, took off for the comfort of the warm bed.

John walked to the nightstand and pulled the phone receiver. Placing his cup of coffee down, he dialed the number and pulled the phone to his ear. Within a few rings, a groggy yet sexy voice answered the phone. "Hello." "Hey, beautiful, wakey, wakey," John said. A cute giggle followed, "Good morning, John." "So did you sleep ok?" John asked. "Well, I was a little restless, but I did get some sleep," Kate answered. "Were you scared?" John asked with an unseen smile, hearing something loud over the phone, in the background. "No, not at all," Kate chirped, sitting up in bed. She had on every light, the T.V., the radio, and had her other hand still locked on a crucifix under her pillow. "Well, that's good! So when should I pick you up?" John asked, taking another sip of his coffee. "Uh, well, can you give me about 20 minutes?" Kate asked as she turned down the volume on her T.V. "You got it! I'll see you soon," John replied. "Ok, bye," Kate said as she hung up the phone and leapt from the bed to get ready. "20 minutes is about an hour on Kate's clock," John whispered as he hung up the phone with a laugh...

There was a settle knock at the door. John could hear the frantic commotion from inside as he waited patiently with a smile. Within a few moments, there was a clatter of locks, and the door suddenly opened. There stood Kate with a smile. "Good morning, John," Kate said, rushing to hug John. "Morning," John replied, hugging her back. John liked the way she felt in his arms, and it kind of scared him. "Ready to go?" John asked, trying to compose himself. "Yep, just let me get my purse," Kate said as she reached just inside the door and pulled her purse from a nearby desk. She walked back out the door and turned to close and lock it. John stood, looking Kate up and down from behind, taking in a sweet smell from her perfume.
"Eric is going to meet us at the lab. He's a phlebotomy technician. He'll help us figure out what we're dealing with. But he's good." Kate said as the two turned and walked to the end of the hall to the elevator. Within a few minutes, the two were on their way to the hospital.

There was a light rap on the door. "Knock, knock," John whispered as he quietly walked into the room. A bright beam of warm sunlight streamed in from the large window onto Preacher's hospital bed and his blanket-covered legs. Slowly, Preacher turned his head and looked at John.

"Hey Brother," Preacher mumbled, not seeming to care. "How are you, Bob?" John asked as he reached Preacher's bedside. A quick yet short smile appeared on Preacher's pale face. "I don't know," he said, shaking his head groggily. "What is it Preacher?" John asked, reaching for his hand.

"I am defeated. God has forsaken me." Preacher mumbled, closing his tired eyes. "Why do you say that?" John solemnly asked, squeezing Preacher's hand softly. "My faith is weak, and it has made him strong," Preacher said, looking out the window, feeling ashamed. "He made me see things... Terrible things... I couldn't sleep. He wouldn't let me. I feel like I'm going crazy. I don't know what's real anymore..." Preacher began to cry.

John moved closer to look Preacher in his tear-filled eyes. "Preacher, look at me," John whispered calmly, yet firmly. Reluctantly, Preacher Bob turned and looked into John's eyes. "Pray with me, Preacher," John said with a tight squeeze to Bob's hand. John's face became stern, and his eyes filled with wrath. He stood straight and began... "God is our refuge and strength, an ever-present help in trouble." Preacher spoke John's words as he pulled himself with John's grasp to sit up straight and continued. "Therefore we will not fear, though the earth gives way and the mountains fall into the heart of the sea, though its waters roar and foam and the mountains quake with their surging."

A sudden chill flowed through Preacher. It was almost electric as his monitors began to hum and beep with the heartbeat and pulse of a young and vibrant man. John smiled, and Preacher smiled back as the sun blazed over the two through the window, and a Heavenly light seemed to envelop the two men.

"Can you feel it, Preacher?" John asked as he felt a rush of Holy energies flow through his body, his arms covered in goose bumps, and unbridled strength in every muscle of his body. "Yes, Brother, I can," Preacher proclaimed, smiling and looking to the ceiling. The brightness of the light began to fade, and a sense of peace fell upon the two men as they embraced. "The Lord is with you, Preacher." "And also with you, Brother John."

The two men smiled at each other.

"You know he is coming back tonight." Preacher said, as he calmly leaned his head back into the soft bed pillow. "I'm counting on it," John replied. "Do you know when and where?" he asked Preacher. "I wish I didn't, but yes, I do. I know things he wants me to know. And he's been messing with my mind, my thoughts. He's trying to drive me crazy, and he's very close to doing so." Preacher whispered in disgust. "Somehow, he got in my head, and I can't get him out." John nodded. "I know Preacher. Victor Delgado is a very powerful monster. I've dealt with him before, a long time ago. He's the reason why I do this." John said as his face twisted in anger.

"You know him, Brother?" Preacher asked, seeing the bitterness in John's face. "Yes, and I've been hunting him down for a long time." John turned away from Preacher and took a few steps to the window. "But it looks like he's found me before I found him," John added. "He thinks you're a threat, Brother. He's afraid. He knows what you're capable of." Preacher said sternly, trying to add to John's confidence. John turned back to Preacher with a smile. "Yeah? And we've got something he wants. And we have to find out why and quick." John walked back over to Preacher's bedside. "Get some rest. Delgado won't bother you during the day as he sleeps." John touched Preacher softly on the back of his hand. I'm going to go down and see how Kate is coming with the blood samples." Preacher nodded and closed his eyes with a smile. "Thank you, Brother John." Within moments, Preacher was deep asleep for some much-needed rest.

Meanwhile, in the hospital's basement lab facility...

Kate and Eric were preparing the collected blood samples for testing as Kate had two separate slides prepared with the feral vampire blood. She placed them under the microscopes. "Ok, well, this may be a first for you and me both," Kate said as Eric pulled up a stool next to her at the second microscope station. "Ok, well, let's see what we've got then," Eric replied, settling into position over the eyepiece. He squinted as he adjusted the zoom into focus on the blood slide. After a moment, Eric's face fell in disbelief as he sat up slowly, trying to process what he had just seen. "Uh, Kate, what exactly is this blood from?" Eric asked with a shaky voice. "Why, what's wrong?" Kate asked. She looked down into her microscope and dialed the optics in for a clear look. Eric waited for Kate's reaction.

"Oh my God," Kate gasped, actually fascinated with what she saw. "Kate," Eric said, waiting for an answer to his question. Kate sat back from the microscope and looked at Eric. "Yeah, that is a little... Different." Kate replied. "Kate, what exactly, are we are looking at?" Eric asked again, becoming agitated. "You wouldn't believe it if I told you," Kate answered, shaking her head. "Try me," Eric shouted, clearly upset at the mystery. "Ok, fine! It's vampire blood." Kate shouted back, expecting Eric to get further frustrated. "Oh, ok," he replied as if it were a rational answer and went back to examining the blood without any further irritations. Kate sat surprised for a moment at Eric's reaction. She shrugged her shoulders and also went back to reviewing the slide of blood.

"Eric, do you have a penlight?" Kate asked, watching the slide of blood. "Yeah, I do. Why?" Eric answered, pulling the light from the pocket of his lab coat. "Well, the cells seem very agitated. I'm thinking it's because of the light maybe," Kate replied as she turned the bright scope light off. She reached up and took the penlight from Eric. Kate looked down into the scope and clicked on the small light. She pulled it closer to the slide until she was able to see. As expected, cell activity significantly settled. Kate then turned on the microscope light and watched as the cells once again broke out into a frenzy of movement.

"Ok, so it doesn't like the light," Kate said as she jotted the info on a form on the clipboard. "Kate, you want a cup of coffee?" Eric asked as he stood up from his station stool. "Sure, thanks," Kate answered as she went back to the looking glass scope. Kate watched the ominous cells, amazed at the structure and its mutated design. "Wow," she thought as she heard Eric walk out through the lab doors.

A sudden scent of fresh coffee caught Kate's attention as she sat up from the lens of the scope. "That was fast," she said as she turned, and out of nowhere, there stood John, holding two cups of coffee with a smile. "John, how did you, I mean, where did you," Kate stuttered slightly startled, but pleasantly surprised. "So, how's it going down here?" John asked, handing Kate a cup carefully. "Well, I'm just fascinated with the vampire's blood. I've never seen anything like it," she answered, blowing on the hot beverage and taking a sip. "Well, let's up the ante," John said, pulling the wax sealed vial of blood from his pocket. "Do you think we can get enough of a sample without actually opening the seal?" John asked, turning the tube in the light. "Well, if I get a big enough needle, we may be able to extract enough of it through the wax and the cork," Kate said, taking another sip of her hot coffee.

Within a few minutes, Kate had readied a large sterile syringe with a long fine needle and taking no chances, outfitted herself with goggles, gloves, a mask, and protective gown. She isolated herself in a small, air-tight glass booth. John stood just outside the enclosure, pouting slightly as he wanted to be the one to retrieve the blood sample, but lost the argument to Kate. She was more qualified, and Eric, who had returned, also voted against John, attempting the possibly dangerous lab work.

Kate carefully placed the sealed tube into a vial rack to hold it secure as she performed the intricate work. "Ok, here we go," Kate said. Very carefully, and with a steady hand, Kate inserted the long needle into the wax and through the cork plug. The needle slowly protruded through the end of the cork and into the crimson fluid. With a pull of the syringe plunger, the barrel began to fill with the red liquid. Kate only took in just enough to sample if indeed, this was a vital fluid that should be preserved. Pulling the needle slowly from the vial, Kate set the syringe carefully on the work platform. She then took a lighter and ignited a flame. Waiving the top of the bottle in front of the fire, the red wax began to become soft, and the small pinhole sealed back over. The vial was again, sealed from any air.

Another quick coffee break, the three were ready to continue their testing on the blood. Eric prepared two more slides as Kate carefully placed a drop of the vialed blood on a slide to examine it by itself before introducing it to the slides of vampire blood.

"Ok, let's see what we've got here," Kate said as she secured the slide to the microscope. Looking into the glass, the three became quiet with anticipation as Kate brought the slide into focus. Kate was quiet...

"Well, Kate," John said, leaning in over her shoulder. Kate's face looked puzzled as she shook her head. "Nothing." Kate sat up and rolled her stool back slightly as Eric leaned into take a look. He stood motionless for a moment as he looked for anything out of the ordinary. "She's right, there's nothing." Eric turned to John, puzzled. "No, there's gotta be something," John said as he made his way in front of Eric and Kate and also looked at the slide. "Hmmm," John mumbled as he also saw nothing. He thought for a moment. "Maybe it's somehow dormant?" John said as Kate and Eric looked at one another. "Well, it is possible, I guess," Eric answered as Kate nodded in agreement.

"We'll find out in a minute," Kate said as she plucked a slide of the vampire blood and carefully applied one small drop of the vialed blood to it. She placed another pane of glass over the slide and centered it to the scope. She gave John a quick look of luck and leaned into focus the lens.

Kate sat motionless for a moment, looking into the scope. She shook her head, "Nope, still nothing. John, I don't... Wait... Something's happening," Kate's voice cracked slightly with excitement. "Oh my God, John, you were right, look, look!" Kate jumped back and pulled John to the scope. "What, what?" John leaned over the scope, not knowing what to look for.

It didn't matter, because John saw the reason for Kate's excitement. He could clearly see the dormant cells becoming active and the vampire cells trying to flee or fight and ultimately being consumed by the vialed cells until the feral cells were completely gone. Eric already had another slide prepared under his scope, also to see the same. He smiled with delight at their test results. "That is amazing," Eric said, sitting back with satisfaction.

"So there's our answer," John said to Kate with a smile as they hugged in celebration. "But we're not done. I want to see how it reacts with human blood and then mix them both with the vampire blood," John said. "Right," Kate said in agreement as Eric gave a snap of his fingers and took off to get more slides.

"Also, I have an idea," John said as he sorted through his thoughts. "Do you have a vial that size and a cork stopper?" "Yeah, why?" Kate asked. John smiled as he thought of his genius mind. "Well, I'll explain it to you. Eric, need more coffee!" John said with excitement. "Right!" Eric turned and headed for the lab door.

By late morning, the blood testing was complete with some surprising results and a few "tricks" that John had come up with, in his back pocket, and an ace up his sleeve. If he was to meet with Delgado, John knew he needed every edge he could find to win any standoff with the Blood Lord Vampire. John's confidence was high, but he knew not to be overconfident.

"Kate, I need you to do me a favor," John said, grasping her shoulder softly. "Of course, what is it?" Kate asked, focusing on John's every word. "Take the vial and hide it, but don't tell me where it is until I ask you for it," John said. "Ok," Kate replied with a confused look. John smiled, "Don't ask, just hide it." Kate smiled back, knowing that John had a method to his madness. "I'm going to go talk to Preacher, and then we can get some lunch, sound ok?" John asked. Kate smiled. "Oh yeah, it does," Kate answered. "I'll clean up and meet you in Preacher's room." John winked and smiled. "See you soon." John turned and walked toward the lab door. "Later, Eric, good work!" Eric looked up from his chart. "Thanks, John! Anything else you need, let me know!" "I sure will," John replied with a smile as he turned through the door.

"Now, you better eat your lunch," Nurse Lisa demanded as she stood with her hands on her hips scolding Preacher. "I told you, I'm not hungry," Bob replied, pushing at the plate. "Now you listen here, preacher man. You've fought me tooth and nail on everything. Now you may be my preacher and a servant of God, but in this hospital, you're in my World! And you're a pain in my fat black ass! So you are going to eat this! And if you don't, I will take this to the kitchen, put it in a blender, puree this shit, and force-feed it to you intravenously! Now, do you understand the words coming out of my mouth?" Nurse Lisa stood dominantly and glared at Preacher.

Without a word, Bob gave Nurse Lisa a dirty look and snatched half of the ham and cheese sandwich from the plate and stuffed the corner of it in his mouth. "There, are you happy now?" Preacher mumbled, chewing with his mouth open. Nurse Lisa smiled. "I will be when I see your empty plate. I'll be back!" Nurse Lisa turned and headed for the door. "Thanks for the warning!" Preacher mouthed back. "Don't push me, preacher man!" Nurse Lisa mumbled as she walked through the door. Frustrated, she didn't even see John standing there as she walked out of the room.

John walked in quietly, looking at Preacher with wide eyes. "And all I have to do is face down a Vampire Lord!" "Brother John! You have to get me outta here before she kills me!" Bob said, grasping for John's open hand. "Bob, we've faced some serious odds, but even if we tried to take her together, I don't think we'd stand a chance! You just better do what she says." John smiled and chuckled at Preacher's predicament with Nurse Lisa. Bob mumbled as he took another bite of the sandwich.

"So Brother, what did you find out?" Preacher asked, wiping his mouth with his napkin. "Well, Bob, I don't want to say too much, not yet," John answered, knowing to limit any information about what they discovered. Delgado could still probe Preacher's mind for anything that he knew and use it against them.

"I understand, Brother. The less I know, the better." Preacher said as John nodded in agreement. "You need to know where he'll be?" Preacher asked poking at a jello cup with a plastic spork. "Yeah." John nodded. "In the church parking lot, at the edge of the cemetery. He'll be there just after sundown." Preacher said reluctantly. "Ok," John said calmly. "I want to come." Preacher said. "I know," John said with a smile. "But not this time, Bob," John commented. Preacher smiled, "I know."

"Hey," A familiar voice came from behind John as Preacher's face lit with a smile. "Kate, a sight for sore eyes. How are you, my dear?" Preacher sat up straight. "I'm good. How are you?" Kate asked, reaching for Preacher's hand. "I'm going to wait out in the hall, Kate, take your time." John interrupted. "Brother," Preacher said, capturing John's attention. "Be careful, good luck, and God be with you." Preacher said softly with a smile. "You bet," John replied with a smile of his own.

John turned and walked out into the hall to wait as Kate visited with Preacher...

$\mathcal{Delgado}$

Chapter Ten

The plan was in place. John was as ready as he could be. Zed was at his side, knowing something big was to happen. Zed could feel that John was uneasy about something, and he would be there the whole way, to support and protect John at all costs. A faithful companion by John's side to the bitter end.

The air was cold yet quiet. A light, flaky snow was falling gently. Now, just a few days before Christmas. It was just before sunset, as John and Zed, patiently waited in the jeep in the church parking lot.

John sat quietly, trying to clear his mind and calm himself from his anger. Zed sat ready, as the darkness of the longest night of the year started to creep over the Dyer landscape. Something suddenly caught Zed's attention as he began a steady low growl. "What you got, bud?" John whispered, knowing Zed's mannerisms all too well. John patted Zed's chest as he looked around the outside of the jeep.

Zed continued to growl softly as he seemed to lock onto something ominous. John's keen night vision just barely caught something out the corner of his eye. Then it was gone. "Ok, bud, it's show time. Stay close, stand fast," John said as he opened the jeep door.

John spun in the driver's seat, swinging his legs out the door as Zed jumped to the driver's side floorboard and leapt to the ground at the same time- a technique they practiced and perfected to ensure each other's safety. They would be side by side at the same time. John closed the jeep door and began to walk toward the center of the lot. Zed matched pace step for step.

As they calmly paced away from the jeep, John caught glimpses of a quickly moving shadow. It seemed to appear at random on all sides of John and Zed. But yet they remained calm and focused. John knew it was a vampire sizing up the two.

"Flank Zed," John quietly commanded. John spread his legs slightly as Zed simultaneously twirled from his side under John's open legs and faced behind. Now, John had a front view, and Zed covered the back. It was now very difficult for the shadow to approach the two unnoticed. Zed began to growl, warning John. But that was also Zed's way of letting John know that he was ready.

A sudden audible whistling tone began to surround the two and resonated through the cold air. John immediately recognized the tune. It was unpleasantly familiar. It was the first few notes of Elvis Presley's "Can't Help Falling in Love." Instead of being a song of love, it was a song of warning and a terrible memory to John.

A look of disgust fell upon John's face as the whistling and shadows continued. John thought of the words of the first verse, "Wise men say, only fools rush in..." Zed's growls intensified. "Bishop, you do remember.." A low, ominous voice said seemingly from all around. "No, I never forgot," John responded with a stern voice. "Why don't you stop hiding like a coward and show yourself?" John snapped, trying to control his rage.

John dropped to his knee, and Zed crouched low to the ground as a rush of frigid air pressed down from above, a roar from an unearthly beast deafened their ears. Then it was quiet.

A towering dark figure stood in their path. Dressed in a medieval black, long-lengthed leather hooded tunic, the fiend stood tall and still. John took a deep breath as Zed came around and stood at John's side to face the creature. Suddenly, the beast opened a pair of glowing yellow eyes and focused on John. "Well, well,

well. It is you, Bishop. It's been a long time," the creature hissed in disgust. "Hello, Victor," John replied, biting his tongue not to say too much, too soon. "You have built up quite the reputation in the Vampire realm." Victor smiled slightly, exposing his fangs. "Almost legendary!" Victor added. "And Zed; God Is Righteousness, a fitting name," the Master vampire looked down to Zed and locked gazes with the K9. Zed stood motionless and fearless.

"No more cat and mouse games, Victor. We won't run." John said confidently, patting the solid body of Zed. The dog slightly wagged his tail, keeping eyes locked on the vampire. "This, I can see, Bishop," Victor said, the smile falling from his pale face. "What do you want?" John asked calmly. "Very simply Bishop, I want the chest and all that it contains. Nothing more, nothing less," the vampire said calmly.

"So, what's in this chest?" John asked as he began the mental chess game. The creature stood tall and tilted his head back slowly, realizing this was not going to be easy. "It is nothing to concern you. It was stolen from me, and now I want it returned. Give me the chest, and I shall leave in peace." Victor said as calmly as he could, although John could detect a hint of impatience in his deep voice.

John grinned at Victor's words. "Well, how do I know it's yours unless you tell me what's in it?" Victor's eyes widened with anger as the creature took a step closer toward John and Zed. Immediately, Zed growled and bared his silver fangs backing the beast. "You don't want any part of him now," John whispered, shaking his head slowly as Zed puffed his fur and spiked the hair on his back.

"Bishop, give me the blood, and I will leave in peace," Victor said, becoming irritated. "Blood? There we go," John said. "So what's the story on the blood?" John asked, feeling his confidence growing. "Where is the blood, Bishop?" Victor asked sternly. "I don't know. But I do know who does know." John smiled as his plan was working perfectly. He knew Victor wouldn't kill him, even if he could. The location of the hidden vial was safe with Kate as John had her hide it and not tell him where.

Victor closed his eyes and sneered, baring his fangs in frustration. Suddenly, the Master vampire stood tall and opened his eyes wide and locked his gaze with John.

Gradually, soft voices began to fill John's head as he tried to fight the hypnotic gaze of the powerful creature. John flinched slightly as a sudden memory flashed through his mind. The voices became increasingly louder as John began to hear screams and see visions of horror running through his mind...

As John and his wife Amy left the nightclub, the night air was warm and pleasant. Hand in hand, they walked through the sparse crowd, which was also leaving and mingling about just outside the club. The thumping dance-tunes resonated between the close buildings as people enjoyed the early evening. The nightlife in the small foreign village was simple and pleasant, and John and his wife were enjoying their honeymoon to the fullest.

There was a sudden high pitched scream that echoed through the air. "What was that?" John said, stopping and turning his head toward the direction of the scream. "What was what?" Amy asked, following John's attention. A few other people stopped as well, trying to locate where the cry came.

A moment later, another chilling scream of terror filled the air. This time, others heard it as well over the nightlife party scene. John took a step with Amy in hand. "It came from over there." Another piercing scream, this time for help, hit John's ear as he now isolated the voice. "Down here," John yelled, releasing Amy's hand as he began to run down a narrow alley. Amy ran behind him, "Go, baby!" she yelled as others joined in the pursuit of the screams. John was at a full sprint, as yet another blood-curdling cry broke through the air. He was a runner and very fast as others tried to catch up with John to help.

John was the first to reach the source of the screaming. It was an enclosed dead-end courtyard in between four buildings. One single street lamp illuminated the area. Dumpsters lined the center of each of the four walls as garbage chutes cast eerie shadows from the random interior lights shining through the clouded windows.

In the center of the courtyard, a towering, dark figure stood. Two massive arms embraced a small framed young woman, her face in a look of complete horror. John ran full bore at the figure as a rush of adrenaline kicked in. "Let her go!" John yelled as he was almost upon the abductor. Suddenly, John froze in his tracks as two glowing yellow eyes locked with his. Amy and several others ran into the courtyard behind John and stopped at the confrontation of the figure.

The pale-faced fiend glanced around at the crowd, drawn in by the screams of his captive victim, and smiled, revealing a set of razor fangs.

"Well, well, well... It looks like we have an audience." The figure's voice was deep and ominous. "How about a sing-along?" People were still trying to process what was happening and what they were seeing. The figure began to sing a verse to a song... "Wise men say... Only fools rush in." A wicked laugh ensued as suddenly seemingly from every direction, fang-bearing fiends began to appear. They were descending from the sky, materializing out of thin air, and crawling down from the sides of the buildings. Vampires were everywhere. It was a trap designed and perfected by the creatures. They would use human empathy and emotions to attract and trap people and prey upon them in a feeding frenzy.

Screams of terror and agony filled the air as blood sprayed everywhere. John turned to see Amy, taunted and laughed at by two of the creatures as she cried out to him, her face crimson red and locked in a look of terror. "Amy!" John yelled, reaching out to her as he couldn't move. He suddenly fell to the ground as a bite to the tender part of the ankle brought him down...

John turned and looked to his heel. Zed was giving him a little chomp. It was enough to break the trance from Victor's powerful hypnotic gaze. "I'm good, bud," John whispered, clearing his head as he realized what had happened.

As if by instinct, John jumped to his feet and produced his silver crucifix to his front. There was Victor, frozen in his tracks as he tried to attack John while he was momentarily down. The vampire pulled his massive forearm to his eyes to protect his sight from the cross. Victor began to cower back slightly. "Only fools rush in," John whispered as he pressed the vampire back. "Ain't that right, Victor?" John said as he reached to the back of his belt with his free hand and unsheathed his silver dagger.

Zed was at John's side, growling and baring his teeth to the vampire, ready to strike at John's command. "You're done, Victor," John said as he sliced at the vampire's forearm. The creature roared in pain as the sharp silver blade sliced through Victor's coat sleeve and across his pale, cold skin. John pressed again with the cross as the vampire dropped his wounded arm from his eyes.

Victor stepped back and began to retreat. "Zed, twilight," John yelled as he stepped forward and stabbed at the creature's bulky frame of a body.

John's blade found its mark in Victor's lower gut as Zed leapt from the ground going airborne. The Master vampire fell back to the ground as Zed's weight toppled the creature. Victor hissed as he tried to fight off Zed, and found his large clawed palm being mauled by Zed's silver fangs and powerful bite.

The vampire continued to thrash about, trying to get to his feet as Zed pressed with his vicious attack. John rushed forward again, dropping the silver dagger into the front of Victor's thick, muscular thigh. The vampire sat up from the sudden intense pain and was able to tear his palm from Zed's vice bite.

John twisted the blade in the creature's leg before pulling it free, causing more damage and pain. Victor swiped at John, catching him across the wrist, knocking the dagger free from John's grasp. As Zed regrouped for another attack, the creature rolled back and to its feet. John still held the crucifix tightly and continued to press Victor backward. The vampire hissed in anger and again gazed sternly at John with his powerful gaze. But John was ready as he pulled a small bottle from his pocket and flung the open neck toward Victor's glowing eyes. A broken stream of Holy water splashed into the creature's open eyes and across his face. The vampire howled in agony as it turned and once again attempted to flee into the darkness. A mist rolled off of Victor from his wounds as he tried to lumber away to safety.

Once again, Zed was on the attack of the retreating creature. The K9 jumped and climbed onto the vampire's hunched-over massive back and viciously bit down into his broad shoulder. Victor instantly dropped to his knee as Zed clamped down and shook violently. The vampire reached over his shoulder and blindly grabbed Zed by the scruff of the neck. With great strength, the vampire ripped Zed from his shoulder and launched the K9 through the air. "Zed," John yelled as he rushed forward to help his companion.

Zed twisted and turned through the air but luckily landed partially in a hedge of soft evergreen bushes. It was enough to break his fall and not cause Zed any severe injuries. Within seconds, Zed was back to his paws and prancing back for another attack on the vampire. "Zed, repent," John commanded as he reached Zed. John turned, and Zed heeled at his side.

Victor was now a safe distance away, severely injured, but still a danger. John and Zed began to walk calmly toward the wounded beast. Feeling confident, John placed the crucifix back into his coat and picked up his dagger from the ground. The vampire stood as tall as he could, trying to gather himself and looked toward the approaching John and Zed. Victor's burning eyes were clouded, and a mist continued to pour from his inflicted injuries of the two hunters.

"Ready for round two, Victor?" John said his dagger at the ready. Zed, with a tail wag, excited to continue the fight. Before John and Zed could attack any further, Victor launched into the air. A trail of black blood followed behind him from his wounds. The vampire was able to elevate himself high enough in a nearby tree. The wounded creature was -at the moment- safe from any further attacks from John and Zed.

"Looks like we're still playing cat and mouse, but this time, the roles are reversed," John said as he placed the dagger back to his belt. "Bishop, I want that blood," Victor growled as his words were labored. "And why do you want the blood, Victor? What's its purpose?" John asked, crossing his arms, waiting for Victor's response. "It is, none of your concern," the vampire struggled with his reply. "Just give me the blood." "And if I don't?" John asked with a smirk.

Anger began to swell within the Master vampire. "Bishop, I will return in two nights. And if you do not hand over the vial, I will bring down a plague upon this town and destroy all that has been rebuilt. Everything you see, everyone you know, will be gone! Give me the blood, and no harm will come." Victor steadied himself on a massive bare limb of the great tree. "That is my promise, and that is my warning. Two nights, Bishop!" With this, the vampire looked to the open sky.

A growl of agony pierced through the cold air. With a short burst of left-over energy, the creature lifted from the tree branch and into the sky. John and Zed stood quietly and watched as the vampire faded into the darkness of the night. Everything was quiet.

As John's adrenaline began to drop, his emotions started to take over. The memories and visions that Victor brought to the surface of his mind overwhelmed John. The images were so vivid, he could hear Amy's cries for help, and he could smell her perfume. John suddenly dropped to his knees and caught his head in the palm of his hands. He began to cry uncontrollably as the visions of that night continued to haunt him.

Zed approached John quietly and solemnly placed his forehead softly to John's neck. Within a few moments, John slowly looked up with tear-filled eyes as Zed softly licked the tears from John's cheek. Zed moved in closer as John laid his head against Zed's soft fur and continued to weep. All Zed could do was comfort his companion and master in his time of need...

Glamour

Chapter Eleven

J ohn quietly parked the jeep a few spaces adjacent to his hotel room door. It was still early in the evening, and the lights were on in his room. John took a deep breath and tried hard to compose himself as he saw a shadow glide across the window.

"Alright, bud come on," John said as Zed stood on the seat, ready to jump from the jeep. John opened the driver's door, and Zed leaped out and ran excitedly toward the hotel room door. John got out, locked the vehicle, and followed Zed as he took a deep breath.

As the two approached the door, it opened, and there was Kate with a smile. Zed pranced inside to greet her, and John followed Zed inside and slightly smiled at Kate. "John, everything ok?" Kate asked, rushing to hug him. "Yeah." John turned and placed his keys on the dresser. Kate could sense something amiss with him. "John, what is it?" Kate asked, looking closely in John's troubled eyes.

John cradled Kate's elbows softly in his hands and sighed. "Everything's fine. I just have to think some things out, that's all." John smiled and kissed Kate gently on the cheek. "I'm going to get cleaned up and then well go get a bite to eat," he said. "Ok," Kate replied as John turned and headed for the bathroom...

The small T.V. surfed from one channel to the next. Preacher mumbled in disgust as he continued to press the remote button looking for something to watch to occupy his wandering attention.

"Good evening Bob," Nurse Lisa said with a sigh, knowing it was just the beginning of her shift with the patient. "Twelve channels and nothing on! Blasphemy!" Preacher clicked off the T.V. and tossed the remote to the side. "Good to see you too, Preacher, and such language," Nurse Lisa said, jotting Bob's stats to her clipboard. "I'm sorry, Nurse Lisa, just a bit restless tonight," Preacher said, wrinkling his face in disgust. "Well, maybe I can get you a little something to take the edge off for you." Nurse Lisa replied, checking Preacher's IV. "That would be a blessing," Bob said with a slight smile. "You just better not give me no headaches tonight, Preacher," she said, bobbling her head. "I promise, I'll try not to," Preacher replied. "Well, at least you'll try not to," Nurse Lisa said, rolling her eyes. "Well, I'll be back," she said, walking toward the door. "It's a little stuffy in here, I'll leave the door open get some air in here." Nurse Lisa opened the door fully and walked out into the hall. Preacher laid his head back to the pillow and closed his eyes. He could hear Nurse Lisa's loud voice carrying down the hall as she joked with her co-workers. It was unexpectedly soothing.

Suddenly, there was a flicker of the lights and a squeal from the monitors. Preacher's eyes snapped open, and he looked around. It was dark and quiet. A few moments later, an auxiliary power came on, and the monitors chirped back to life. The low wattage light above his bed flickered back on. Preacher sat up slowly and peered out the open door and into the dimly-lit hall. It seemed that there was a power outage, and only a grid or two of power came on from the generators. But all was strangely quiet. Preacher looked around and listened carefully for any voices from the staff on duty, but heard no one. The only thing he could hear was a slight whistle from the wind outside. Preacher took a breath and tried to remain calm, laying his head back down onto his pillow. He slowly looked around the semi-dark room and didn't notice anything out of the ordinary.

Suddenly, Preacher's ears picked up on something down the hall. There was a slight sharp squeak, then a short shuffle. Preacher looked out the door and sat up quietly as again, he heard a squeal followed by a shuffle.

Whatever the source of the noise was, it was coming from down the hall. And it was coming slowly. Again, Preacher heard the squeak followed by a short shuffle. He reached down and nervously pressed the button for the nurse with a shaky hand. His heart rate began to race as the monitors began to chirp erratically.

Again, a screech and a shuffle, this time, it seemed to be just outside the door of Preacher's room. "Come on, nurse, where are you," Preacher whispered, breaking into a slight cold sweat. The squeak again, and then the shuffle caught Preacher's jumpy attention. He looked out the open room door. Just outside in the hall, sat a mobile IV drip stand.

"Nurse Lisa, is that you?" Preacher asked with a shaky voice. Just then, the IV stand moved forward with a squeaky wheel, then the shuffle. Preacher's eyes widened as he now saw who was pushing the mobile IV stand. A patient stood quietly, grasping onto the IV cart with an extended arm. Dressed in a loose hospital gown, and wearing a pair of worn brown slippers. The patient's head was down, staring at the floor. Long, scraggly, and thin curly blonde hair dangled from its head, covering its face.

"Hello, are you ok out there?" Preacher asked. The figure stood quiet and motionless just outside the doorway in the dimly lit hallway. No response came. "I think the power went out from the wind, but I just called for the nurse. She's on her way." The patient suddenly pushed the IV stand with a stout squeak and a short, fast shuffle. Preacher jumped slightly, as again the figure stood still and silent at the center of the open door.

"What's your name?" Preacher asked, trying to remain calm. "I'm Preacher Bob," he added with a slight chuckle. Slowly, the patient began to turn its head toward Preacher. The sound of stiff bones cracking and popping reached Preacher's ears as he became more unsettled. As the figure's head turned, its hair fell away from its twisted face. "Oh no, not again, Lord," Preacher whimpered, his lips began to tremble.

A labored gasp and gurgle came from the figure as it shifted and turned to enter the room. A squeak and a shuffle, as it stumbled forward into the room. Preacher screamed in terror as the dim light revealed a decomposing corpse, exposed bones, grey rotting flesh, and a stench of death.

"Oh my God in Heaven, you're not real! You are not real!" Preacher yelled, scrambling to lower the bed railing on the opposite side of the hospital bed. The animated corpse shuffled forward, its mouth gaping open as its bony hand held the IV stand tight in its grasp to steady itself.

Preacher flew into a panic; his heart and pulse monitor began to scream with audible alarms. Try as he might, he could not get the bed rail to release. The corpse again moved closer, reaching out with its free hand to grab Preacher. "Back to Hades with thee in the name of God, I command you!" Preacher screamed, trying to hold his voice in a commanding tone.

Preacher reached down and retrieved the bed remote and wildly began to press buttons in panic. The corpse now grabbed the bed rail and shuffled another step forward. The bed started to lower down as the rotting corpse's pitted empty eye sockets stared down over Preacher.

The corpse leaned over the railing but could only bend down so far from rigor mortis. Preacher froze in horror as the zombie attempted to bite through the air at him. Preacher closed his eyes and took a breath as it seemed like he was out of danger for the moment. It was short-lived however, as suddenly the bed began to rise. Through his panicked pressing of the remote buttons, it placed the bed into reset mode. The bed continued to lift closer and closer, the corpse's jaw snapped at Preacher, repeatedly.

Preacher screamed as he raised his arm to shield himself from the fiend's attack. As the distance closed, the corpse's jagged teeth sank deep into Preacher's exposed forearm. Preacher closed his eyes and cried out in agony. Blood sprayed everywhere, as the corpse's powerful bite ripped the flesh from his arm.

Preacher opened his eyes to see the corpse chewing delightfully on the piece of flesh as his arm spewed blood everywhere from a severed vein. Suddenly, a hand came into view over the shoulder of the monster.

"Carl, how did you get out of your room?" a familiar voice broke through the chaos. Preacher blinked wildly, glancing around. There was Nurse Lisa, pulling and turning a man in a hospital gown away from the side of Preacher's bed. "Sorry about that, Preacher. Looks like Carl here broke out of the ward again. Come on, Carl. Say "goodbye" to Preacher." The man stopped, turned, and waived at Preacher. "Bye," the child-minded man said with a giggle as Nurse Lisa guided him toward the door. "I'll be back with your dinner, Preacher. Come on, baby," the nurse said as she carefully guided Carl and his IV stand out the door and down the hall.

Preacher's bed finally stopped lifting. He quietly looked around, and everything was back to the way it was. His arm was fine; there was no blood and the power and lights were back on. He could hear the voices of people out in the hall. Preacher sat back and closed his eyes. As he did, he saw a flash of glowing yellow eyes and heard a sinister laugh in his head. Preacher flinched as his eyes sprang open from the vision and the voice. "I can't take much more of this Devil shit," he mumbled, pulling his Bible to his chest from a nearby table. He began to weep from the constant torment...

John stood, seemingly frozen, looking down at his bloodied hands. A chaotic scene was playing out all around him. He led people down an alley, and now, they were all trapped. Being ravaged and torn apart in a feeding frenzy. No matter how fast they ran, or where they went, or how hard they each fought. They were no match for the creatures of the night.

John could hear the words clearly, "Wise men say, only fools rush in." The bloodied bodies fell to the ground and flew through the air. Blood and lifeless bodies were everywhere. The creatures laughed and mocked the people running and begging for their lives. Some began to cry for help themselves as more people began to filter down the dead-end alley to answer the cries. It was a perfect trap. More people came, as more vampires appeared.

John turned and began to run toward two of the creatures that had Amy trapped. They were tormenting her and laughing with delight, like two cats playing with a mouse. John reached one of the vampires and pulled the creature to face him. With all of his strength, John punched the monster in the jaw. A perfect punch turned the creature's head slightly and dislodged its jaw, but the beast still stood.

The vampire reached to its broken jaw and reset it in place without even a flinch. Before John could do anything further, the fiend pulled back and answered John's punch with a powerful backhand of its own. John's limp body flew head over heels through the air and slammed into the side of a dumpster denting and moving it slightly. As John slipped into unconsciousness, all he could see was Amy screaming in terror as the two vampires rushed in and bit viciously into her flesh...

John sat up suddenly and swung his feet out of the bed and to the floor. He sat covered in a cold sweat, breathing heavily from the vivid visions of the nightmare. John leaned forward and dropped his head into the open palms of his hand as he began to weep quietly. He could still smell the sweet perfume Amy had on that tragic night.

The covers began to stir behind John in the bed. "John," a soft voice touched his ears. Kate sat up quietly in the darkness pulling the sheet and bunching them up around her naked body. "Yeah," John responded calmly, trying to slow his breathing.

"What's wrong?" Kate asked solemnly as she quietly shuffled across the bed on her knees and carefully reached through and embraced John's sweated chest from behind. "I'm ok, Kate," John said, wiping the tears from his eyes. He reached over to the bedside light as he felt Kate's soft hair brushing over his shoulder. "John," Kate whispered in his ear to calm him as she embraced him in her arms. John clicked the light on and turned to face Kate with a warm smile.

John's eyes widened as Kate reared back, her eyes glowing, face twisted with a gaping mouth of razor fangs. Before John could react any further, Kate bolted forward and bit down into John's bare shoulder like a ravaged animal. John winced in pain and froze in shock as crimson blood spewed everywhere.

John sat up suddenly and swung his feet out of the bed and to the floor. "What the fuck," John whispered as he sat in a cold sweat breathing heavily. He glanced around in the darkness. Everything was calm and quiet, other than the familiar broken snoring of Zed from the corner of the bed.

There was a stir in the bed behind him. "John," a soft voice touched his ears. Kate sat up quietly in the darkness pulling the sheet and bunching them up around her naked body. "Yeah," John responded calmly, trying to slow his breathing.

"What's wrong?" Kate asked solemnly as she quietly shuffled across the bed on her knees and carefully reached through and embraced John's sweated chest from behind. "I'm ok, Kate," John said, taking in a deep breath as he felt Kate's soft hair brushing over his shoulder. "John," Kate whispered in his ear to calm him as she leaned over and reached for the bedside light.

Kate clicked on the light and turned to face John with a warm smile. Her eyes widened in horror as John's glowing eyes locked with hers. John's wicked face smiled with a mouth of dripping razor fangs. Kate let out a blood-curling scream as John unhinged his jaw and viciously bit down into Kate's neck as warm blood sprayed everywhere.

John sat up suddenly and swung his feet out of the bed and to the floor. "Fuck!" John said as he sat in a cold sweat, breathing heavily. He glanced around in the darkness. Everything was calm and quiet, other than the familiar broken snoring of Zed from the corner of the bed.

The covers began to stir behind John in the bed. "John," a soft voice touched his ears. Kate sat up quietly in the darkness pulling the sheet and bunching them up around her naked body. She reached over on her side and clicked on the bedside light.

Immediately, John jumped from the bed and reached for his silver dagger on the bed stand. He turned to face Kate with the blade ready in his grasp. "Oh my God, John," Kate screamed, cowering back in fear as she saw the look on John's face.

John stood, a look of rage on his face. He tightened his grip on the hilt of the dagger as he slowly began to move toward Kate. All he could see was a vampire that needed to be killed. Again Kate tried to get through to John. "Baby, it's me, Kate!" She looked and saw John's eyes were coal black.

John's stance steadied as he continued to move forward with his dagger at the ready. "You're gonna die, just like the rest of them, you blood-sucking bitch!" Kate pulled the pillow to her front as she scrambled to move out of harm's way. "John, please, no!" Kate screamed.

Suddenly, Zed leapt onto the bed and placed himself between John and Kate. Zed stood, calm, looking at John and knew he wasn't himself. Zed could feel it.

Zed stood ready as John continued to advance. Kate rolled out of bed and onto her feet, just as John raised the dagger to attack. Like a bolt, Zed powerful legs launched the K9 into the air and at John. Kate screamed as John and Zed dropped behind the side of the bed in a tangled heap.

Kate gasped as all she could see was an arm holding a knife and a tail and fur as the two wrestled. Then John yelled as Zed yelped. Then all was quiet. Kate feared the worst as she quietly crept around the front of the bed.

As she slowly made her way around the bed, there was John's dagger lying on the carpet. Another step and she saw John's foot. Kate sighed a breath of relief. She came around to see John, on his back. Zed was sprawled over the top of him, licking his face excitedly as John rubbed the dog's massive head playfully, with a smile.

"We're ok, Kate. We're ok," John said as he playfully pushed Zed off to the side. John pulled himself up to his feet and walked to Kate. She could see the tears filling in his eyes. "Kate, I am so sorry," "It's ok, John," she said as the two embraced tightly. "It wasn't me," John whispered in her ear. "I know it wasn't, babe, I know," Kate replied as a tear rolled down her cheek. "It's ok, John," she added as she kissed John passionately on the lips wiping the tears from his face...

'Twas the Night Before Crimson

Chapter Twelve

T he morning was early in Dyer. The air was crisp, and the sun was shining. The entire town seemed inlaid with diamonds as all of the frosted surfaces glistened in the sunlight. There was light traffic on the roads as people mingled about starting the day.

A jeep pulled off the main road and into the lot of the small specialty garage. John parked and turned off the engine. With his eye patch in place, keeping his left eye trained for the dark times to come, John exited the jeep and headed for the front door of the business.

John pushed the door open as a bell jingled. A moment later, a tall skinny man with a well-groomed mullet walked through a back service door and appeared behind the parts counter. "Morning, sir, welcome to Custom Corner. How can I help you today?" the man asked as he took a sip of steaming coffee. "Yes, I'm looking for Ed," John said as he stopped at the counter. "You found him. I'm Ed," the man answered, placing his coffee cup to the bench. "Ed, I'm John, I called you yesterday..." "...about the remote start," Ed interrupted. "Yes," John said with a smile.

"Ah, is that it out there?" Ed asked, coming out from behind the counter to take a closer look at John's wheels through the window. "Yep, that's it," John replied. "Oooooo-weee! Man, you got that sucker suped-up! That is nice," Ed said, almost seeming to drool. "Well, I got the remote starter in stock and can get right on it." "Can I wait on it?" John asked. "You sure can. It's a little bit of a wait though," Ed added. "How long are you looking?" John asked, pulling the keys from his pocket. "Eh, if all goes well, about two and a half hours," Ed replied, holding his hand out to John to retrieve the keys. "Ok, I'll go next door to get a bite to eat. Take your time," John said with a smile dropping the keys into Ed's open palm. "No problem, man," Ed said, whistling a Skynyrd tune, tossing the keys in his hand as he turned to go back behind the counter and through the service door.

John walked out of the shop entrance, and a side garage door began to open. John threw a settle wave as Ed came out from under the door to get John's jeep. John turned and jumped the curb walking toward the near-by diner to get a bite to eat.

A waitress opened the door for John as he approached. She just got done cleaning the smudges off the glass door. "Good morning, sir. How are you today?" the waitress asked, as John entered with a smile. "I am good, how are you?" he replied. "Good, thank you," the waitress said with a return smile. "Please have a seat and someone will be right with you," she added, collecting the bottle of blue Windex and her cleaning rag. "Thanks so much," John said as he walked toward a booth.

John stopped momentarily and glanced around. Something was familiar. "Holy shit," John mumbled as a sudden flash of a bloody violent scene flashed in his head. John walked over and slowly slid into a short booth along the wall. Another flash of a previous terror-filled vision entered his head. John now recognized this place as the former Cullie's Diner. John looked out the window and saw the sign now read, Cassie's Diner. He could still see the "U, L, L" slightly, under the new letters, "A, S, S" as he chuckled under his breath.

The diner had been remodeled, and the massacre, painted and wallpapered over, unbeknownst to most of the patrons. John glanced up, and his uncovered eye focused on a crack in the thick glass of the windowpane. It had attempted to be repaired and just covered up with a strip of tinted film and a cheap set of short curtains. But John knew how the crack came to be, from the violent attack on the Dyer Police officers that took the call that tragic night.

John took a quick observation of the diner. People were trickling in from the cold for their morning shots of coffee and hot plates of breakfast. There were settle hints of Christmas from Holiday decorations scattered about.

Dyer itself was a small town that was growing, changing. But John knew the ancient little village had its share of scars, hidden mysteries, and tarnished bits of history about it.

"Oh, my God! John Bishop!" A startled voice captured John's wandering mind. John turned and looked up at a familiar face, but the name slipped his mind for a moment. "I'm Nancy, Nancy Thompson." The waitress pointed to her name badge as she smiled. "Nancy, my God, how are you, my dear?" John said, smiling back as he looked at a strand of silver hair which was prominent against her tied-back brown hair. "I'm ok," Nancy replied, turning her head of silvered hair from John's view from embarrassment.

John pulled his eye to hers. "You never left Dyer?" John asked as he sat back, intrigued. Nancy hesitated for a moment. "No," she shook her head. "My dad got promoted to Lieutenant on the Dyer Police force after what happened, and then we move to a new subdivision on Elm Street. But we're still here in Dyer." Nancy smiled and laughed nervously. "Well, it's good to see you, Nancy," John said, smiling. "How about a cup of coffee and a strawberry Danish?" he added. "Of course," Nancy said with a sigh and a smile. She turned and walked toward the counter to get John's order.

John's mind began to wander once more as he began to hear the settle cries of Nancy and Faith - the other waitress that was on duty that horror-filled night at the diner. But Nancy was still there. After what she witnessed that night, John knew this was a testament to Nancy's inner strength. She was a fighter, and the silver in her hair was but just a scar.

John also knew Nancy could overcome any nightmare, as he could.

Moments later, Nancy returned with a pot of fresh coffee and a large strawberry Danish on a small plate. "Hot and fresh for you," Nancy said with a smile. "Wonderful," John replied as he took the pastry plate, reaching over and flipping the coffee cup from the table placemat. Carefully, Nancy poured the coffee and reached into her apron pocket to get a couple of cream cups. "Anything else I can get you?" Nancy asked. "No, I'm good, thanks," John replied. "Hey, where's Zed?" Nancy asked, concerned. "Oh, he's back at the hotel, still sleeping. He's not an early riser." Nancy giggled at John's remark. "Well, can you give him a cookie for me?" she asked, pulling a dog biscuit from her pocket and holding it to John. "Well, I'll tell you what," John said, gently clasping Nancy's hand. "How about you give him a cookie yourself? I'll bring him over for you." Nancy's face lit with happiness. "That would be so cool," she said with a smile. "Merry Christmas, Nancy," John said, gracefully flipping his hand with the skill of a well-trained magician. Nancy's eyes grew wide as now there was a $100 bill between his fingers. "That's for the Danish, coffee, and you." Nancy gratefully took the money from John. "Thank you, John," she said with a big smile and slightly red face. She placed the money in her apron, turned, and almost started to cry from John's generosity as she walked away.

As John enjoyed his Danish and sipped on his coffee, a particular noise captured his attention. John's keen hearing dialed onto someone walking from the back of the diner. Someone wearing cowboy boots, walked with a limp and a slight drag across the tiled floor because of a bad leg. It was very distinct to John, as he knew it well.

"Well, I'll be Goddamn! It is you." John turned his head, and a middle-aged scruff of a man stood glaring at him. His long straggly white hair partially covered his bearded face as his piercing blue eyes seemed to stare intensely at John.

"Abraham, I knew that was you. How are you, my friend?" John said calmly with a smile. "Been better, been worse. I could complain, but no one would give a shit," the man grumbled, sliding into the empty booth seat across from John. "How are you,

Bishop?" "I could say the same," John replied, taking another sip on his cup of coffee. "How's the pup?" Abraham asked, settling into the worn cushions of the red vinyl booth seat. "He's good," John said with a slight nod. "How are those silver fang implants holding up?" the man asked, staring keenly at John. "Very well, I have to say. We just keep them sharp and polished. Keeps them very effective and makes him look damn cool." Abraham smiled at John's answer.

"So, what brings you to Dyer?" John asked as he took a bite of Danish. "I got a lead on a bloodsucker I've been tailing across three states. Got word that something big is going down here in Dyer." Abe leaned in with a slight grin. "This wouldn't happen to be a party that you're hosting, would it?" John picked up his napkin and wiped at his lips, giving a slight "wink" at the man. "You somebitch! You mean you would have a party and not invite me?" John laughed at Abe's remark. "When in Hell's fire did you ever need an invite to a party? You're the biggest party crasher I've ever known." John added with an evil smile. "Well, you're right there," Abe replied with a chuckle.

Abe tilted his head and took a glance across the diner. "So, who's the guest of honor?" John's face fell into an intense frown as he sat quietly for a moment. "Delgado," John said sternly as his uncovered eye intensely locked with Abe. "Delgado," Abe sat up straight. "How the Hell did you hook into that big fish?" John took a deep breath to calm himself. "He actually found me. I've got something he wants." Abe sat silent as a patron passed by the booth.

"When and where, I'll be there," Abe said, tapping steadily on the table. "You bring Zed, God, and the thunder, and I'll bring the guns and bullets," he said with a smile. "No, this is personal," John growled slowly. Abe's tapping fingers stopped. "Personal? Well, if someone knows personal, it's me." Abe knew, like all hunters, when an encounter with a vampire was called personal; it was just that and marked as such.

John cleared his throat and took another breath to calm down. "So, what have you been up to besides chasing down suckers?"

John asked, changing the subject. "Well, I've been working on a new..." Abe hesitated for a moment before continuing. "Protégé." John's brow rose with interest. "Really?" he replied. "Yeah, he's a work in progress. But damn, unlimited potential. Got a few bugs to work out of him, but put a blade in his hands, unstoppable—a real game-changer." Abe smiled at the thought.

"You ever going to get rid of that old jacket?" John asked, looking at a slice of tattered leather hanging from one of the sleeves of Abe's black jacket. "You ever going to stop wearing that dumbass eye patch?" Abe replied with a smirk. "You ever going to stop being an asshole?" John remarked back. "Never," Abe replied sternly. Both men began to laugh.

"No, this old jacket is like me- getting old but never going out of style." John smiled softly at Abe's remark, taking another sip of coffee. "Besides," Abe sat up. "There are a lot of memories attached to this jacket." Abe dropped his head and took a breath. "Like the time we were out riding, and we stopped at that roadside bar in the middle of nowhere." John nodded as he began to remember. "We got drunk and didn't realize we were in a bar full of vampires," Abe said as John fell back in the booth and began to laugh hysterically. "How the Hell did we survive that one?" John asked, shaking his head in disbelief. "Well, it helped that they were a little bit drunker than we were." Both men began to laugh at the memory of that night. As their laughter faded, they both sat quietly for a moment.

"Every little thing we do, makes a difference in this," Abe said quietly. "Yes, it does," John said, giving a slight nod of agreement. Abe shook off the feelings of reminiscence and sat up straight. "So, you and Zed got this?" Abe asked, focusing on John's answer. John squared himself up and looked confidently at Abe. "Yeah."

"Ok, then." Abe nodded and brought his hand up over the table. John raised his hand and locked wrists in the air with Abe in a powerful mutual grip. "Good luck," Abe said solemnly with a smile. "You to Brother," John replied, smiling back.

"Well, I'm out." Abe released his grip and slid out of the booth and to his feet. "Good to see you, Bishop." John nodded in agreement. "You too." "I'll see you down the road," Abe said with a fake smile. "You bet," John added with a mustered smile of his own. Both men stood and stared at each other for a moment. Both knew this could very well be the last time they would ever see each other alive. It went with the nature of their cause.

Abe dropped his head, turned, and limped toward the door. "Merry Christmas, Abe," John said. "Unless you have a family, Christmas doesn't mean shit," Abe barked as John chuckled, expecting nothing less. "You too, asshole," Abe mumbled, reaching the door. The door jingled as Abe walked outside.

John walked over to the small lot as Ed was just backing the jeep out of the garage. Ed smiled at John through the windshield as he pulled the vehicle up next to where John was standing, slightly revving the engine. Ed turned off the engine and stepped out as John walked up. "Man, oh man, that is a sweet ride," Ed remarked as he handed John the keys.

"Thanks," John said with a smile, looking at the new key fob in his hand. "Because it's Christmas, I went ahead and gave you the deluxe upgraded model for no extra charge." "Hey, thanks," John said gratefully. "No problem, man! I forgot I just got the deluxe kits in last week. It's got a few extra features on it, and it's the latest and the greatest!" "So, what's the range on the remote?" John asked. "Eh, I'd say between 30 to 70 feet. It really depends on the battery, the weather, if you're inside, going through walls, that sort of thing." Ed replied, tapping on a can of Skoal tobacco. "Perfect," John said as he thought of things to come.

"Well, come on in, and I'll get you a receipt," Ed said, pulling his shop rag to wipe his smudged hands. "Sounds good," John said as the two men walked toward the shop door.

Back at the hospital...

It was mid-morning as the sun shined brightly through the window of the hospital room. The T.V. was on with an episode of "The Price is Right." Bob Barker was warning one of the contestants just called from their seat. A hefty woman was screaming and jumping in excitement from being, "the next contestant." The woman stood at the podium with a broad smile, "Hi, Bob Barker," the woman squealed. Bob Barker stood quiet for a moment with a slight grin. The audience began to laugh. "You are a Samoan, aren't you?" Bob asked. "Right, I am Samoan," the woman said, laughing as the audience began to laugh and clap. Bob glanced up at the camera. "This is the fourth one," he said, the crowd hollered out in laughter. "I have had a great deal of trouble with Samoans." Another laugh from the crowd as the woman smiled. "Open your jacket, let me see your name there," Bob said, leaning in as the woman opened her blue jacket. "Nus.. Nus," he stuttered. "Nussolia," the woman said slowly. "Nussolia," Bob said as the woman nodded, "Right," she added. "Have you seen the other Samoans on the show?" Bob asked. "Right, I seen the lady. She's carry you up," the lady said, getting excited as she laughed and clapped. The audience responded with a roar of laugher. Bob stood quiet with a smile as the backstage announcer broke out in laughter. "You thought that was fun?" Bob said as the woman began to laugh and clap once more. "You thought that was fun?" Bob asked sternly again. "Hmm? Did you think that was fun?" Bob asked once more. "Yes, it's fun," she replied as she and the audience began to laugh and clap again. "Alright," Bob sighed, getting back to the show.

"If she wins, Brother's going to get tossed around like a rag doll!" Preacher Bob mumbled as he laughed at the prospect. "Knock, knock," Preacher turned, and there was Kate at the door with a warm smile.

"Kate, my dear, an angel from Heaven," Bob said with his preacher's bellow. Kate walked in closer, smiling. "So how's Preacher Bob this morning?" "Doing much better, my dear. And you, oh my, my, my. Kate, you are just glowing in the sunlight. And your smile! I bet John is smiling brightly this morning as well," Preacher commented as Kate began to blush.

"Where is Brother John this morning?" Bob asked as Kate stopped at the side of the bed. "He's getting something done to the jeep," Kate said, as Bob nodded understandingly. "Speaking of John, something happened last night," Kate said. "Oh, I bet it did," Preacher replied with a smile. "No, I mean, something..." Kate hesitated a moment. "...Unsettling, happen last night." a look of concern fell over Kate.

Preacher knew by the look in Kate's eyes, something was wrong. "Well, what is it, child?" Bob asked, sitting up slightly as he turned down the volume on the T.V. "John awoke from a nightmare and pulled his knife on me." Kate struggled with the unbelievable words. "What?" Bob whispered, reaching for Kate's hand. "He wasn't himself, and his eyes looked black. And he saw me as a threat. Preacher, he wanted to kill me." Kate's lips began to quiver as a single tear rolled down her cheek. "Kate, take heed child. That wasn't John," Preacher whispered calmly.

"John has been infected with evil, as I have," Bob said, closing his eyes in disgust. "What do you mean?" Kate asked, standing still. "Delgado." Kate's mouth dropped at Bob's response. "Kate, Delgado is a bad, bad, minion of evil. Very wicked. Very powerful. After my encounter with him, it's been pure Hell." "What do you mean?" Kate asked, focusing on Preacher's words.

"Once he's... in your head, he can control your thoughts, senses, and make you see things." Preacher sat back as he tried to explain the torment. "Every night, I've had to deal with unspeakable horrors that seem so real, but they are not. And even though you know it's not real, it is still tough to overcome. And John, John, has been infected by the same torment." Kate's eyes filled with tears. "I'm so sorry, Preacher," she said, kissing his hand gently.

"But John has been affected so much more deeply," Bob said solemnly. "Why is that?" Kate asked, concerned. Preacher took a deep breath. "He confided in me, and that is for him to explain to you, not me. But his life was affected deeply by Delgado long ago." Kate wiped the tears from her eyes as she came to terms with what Preacher had told her.

"But John and Zed are going to destroy Delgado, right?" Kate asked Bob looking for reassurance. Preacher smiled softly. "I say yes," his face fell as he continued. "But in my heart, I don't think he can." Kate stood silent for a moment...

"There's got to be something, something we can do," Kate said. "We need to help John." "I know, dear, but even if we could, we could only do so much. In the end, John is the only one who can defeat the demons that plague him. We all have our own personal demons, and Delgado is his," Preacher said quietly, staring into Kate's tear-filled eyes. "But there just may be something we can do to help John," Preacher added with a smile. Kate smiled back as the two began to scheme.

John pulled the jeep into the lot and parked in front of his hotel room. Zed excitedly peeked out from behind the window curtain, hearing the familiar rumble of the jeep's high-performance exhaust. It was early afternoon, and the sun was already on its way down, as was the air temperature.

John jumped from the jeep, pulling a bag of five plain hamburgers out with him from McDonald's as he shut the door. Zed's eyes focused on the bag as John approached. John began to laugh, "What?" he said as he lifted the bag and shifted it from side to side. Zed's eyes locked onto the bag and followed it with every twitch of John's arm. Zed's head seemed to vaporize from the window as John opened the room door.

John disappeared behind the closed door, and Zed pranced with excitement. "Damn, boy! Looks like you're more excited to see a McDonald's bag than you are to see me! Ok, ok.. Let's see what we have." Zed, stood, his face locked in a pose of an open drooling jaw. John smiled, holding the bag open. "Oh no," he sighed with a sad look. Zed's head cocked over at John's reaction. "Well, sorry, bud. I had some food, but it's gone." Zed's jaw closed, and he stood silent. John dropped the bag in front of Zed on the floor. Eagerly, Zed stuck his snout into the neck of the bag and wrestled the edge open with his nose and tongue. An irritated grunt and snort came from Zed as he stuck his head deeper into the hamburger scented baggie.

John laughed under his breath at the sight of Zed standing

motionless with his head completely buried in the paper bag. Other than the smell of fresh burgers, the bag was empty. Slowly, Zed pulled his head from the bag until only his eyes were visible and staring wickedly at John.

Zed began to growl at John's trickery. "Ok, ok. You got me, come on." John turned and produced one wrapped burger after another from his pockets. "It's hydrate time," John said as Zed jumped onto the bed. John opened the wrappers and placed the food in front of the K9. Zed's tail wagged, chomping joyfully on the burgers. John pulled an IV from a nearby duffle. It was a carefully mixed concoction of saline, blessed water, garlic, and colloidal silver. It made for a very unpleasant experience for a vampire, if it was to bite into the IV recipient.

John hung the bag at the top of the bed headboard and attached the tube and needle to the IV bag. Carefully, John took a paw from Zed and inserted the needle as he pinched the skin. Zed never flinched as he continued to enjoy the burgers. "I'll get mine in a bit, but first a nice hot tub," John whispered to himself.

With Zed comfortable, John made his way to the bathroom as he began to shed his clothes. John walked into the bathroom, and the floor tile was cold on his bare feet. He turned the spigot and pulled the stopper as the tub began to fill with hot water.

Wrapped in a towel, John kneeled, closed his eyes and began to pray next to the filling tub of water. As he spoke the Holy words, the water began to sparkle and take on Heavenly properties. Moments later, John turned off the water and stood. He hung the towel on a nearby hook and stepped into the tub. Slowly, John slid down into the hot bath and closed his eyes with a calming sigh. He could instantly feel the tension, aches, and pains, and mental uncertainty leave his body. His troubled soul and well being began to calm as his thoughts became organized and clear. The water glistened and sparkled against his skin. Peace filled his body.

The hotel room door opened as Zed raised his head from a quick nap. "Hey Zed," Kate whispered, closing the door behind her.

Zed's tail wagged a few times as he lowered his head back to the soft bed as his IV was at half-drip.

Kate placed her keys on the dresser and called out softly, "John?" Kate quietly made her way to the bathroom door, which was slightly ajar. "John?" she whispered as she pushed the door open and walked into the mist-filled room.

It was quiet. Kate walked into the bathroom and saw the curtain pulled closed around the tub. "John," Kate said as her mind began to worry. She stood next to the tub and gulped as she reached over and grasped the far edge of the shower curtain. Slowly with a shaky hand, Kate began to pull the curtain back. As she did, there was no sound, and she could see John's motionless feet and legs.

"John," she said louder, becoming worried as she continued to pull on the curtain. Kate closed her eyes and prepared for the worst, as the curtain cleared the tub to the side. She opened her eyes to John's still body, his face covered with a blue washcloth, the tub water as still as could be.

"John," she said quietly as she leaned in closer. Still, no movement, no response. Slowly she reached over and pinched the edge of the washcloth and began to pull it from John's covered face. Still nothing.

Kate's heart began to race as she lifted the cloth. "John, please say something." The washcloth lifted, and John's eyes closed- a peaceful look upon his face. Kate stood, waiting for a response, still nothing. She leaned in closer to see if John was breathing. Kate could not see his chest moving at all. She reached down and grasped around John's wrist, his arm lying on the edge of the tub. She felt for a pulse and concentrated quietly. Nothing...

"Oh my God," Kate whispered, standing up straight as she turned to collect herself to perform C.P.R. Suddenly, John's hand reached out and grabbed Kate's wrist in a secure yet gentle hold and began to pull her back.

Kate let out a slight scream of surprise as she found herself being pulled over the edge of the tub and into the warm water. Her scream faded into a soft giggle as she felt John reaching through her arms and pulling her into a secure embrace as the water soaked through her clothes.

Kate turned and looked into John's eyes as he smiled softly. "Boo," he whispered, staring intently in Kate's eyes. "John Bishop, what am I going to do with you?" Kate asked as she began to let herself mesh softly with John.

As the warm water saturated around her body, Kate felt all doubts and fears fade away. A clarity and a peace came over her, unlike anything she had ever felt. "Oh my God, John, what is happening?" Kate asked, staring into John's eyes. "It's the power of the Heavens and all that is good," John replied calmly.

Kate leaned forward and held John's face in the palm of her hands. She gently kissed John on the lips as his hands slowly move down her shoulders, to her back, and down into the back pockets of her soaked jeans. Kate smiled and sat up, pressing on John's muscular chest. She reached down and grabbed the edge of her shirt and pulled it up, over and off, tossing the soaked shirt to the floor. A settle giggle followed as she reached into the water and unsnapped a button and pulled down the zipper on her jeans.

A smile stretched across John's face. With the front of Kate's jeans undone, she leaned forward and arched her back. John pressed down into the pockets, and Kate slid out of the jeans revealing a soaked red thong suctioned to her supple, water-beaded skin. A moment later, a pair of wet jeans plopped onto the bathroom floor, followed by a drenched bra and panty set. For the two, at that moment, it was complete euphoria as the two slid into the tub of soothing Holy water...

The Reckoning

Chapter Fourteen

The door opened, and there stood John. Dressed head to toe in black, wearing a long-lengthen leather coat. As if prepared for battle, assorted weapons and Holy trinkets lined the inside of the jacket in hidden pockets, loops, and up sleeves. His cane, to one side, and his K9 on the other, John was ready.

His head was clear, calm, and collected. His plan was in place, although it was just that. Filled with many variables and directions it could go. And the outcome, unclear. But as ready as he could be. His plan for Kate, to be at the hospital with Preacher and be prepared in case things went south. Little did John know, Kate and Preacher had worked a plan to help John. So only God knew the outcome of what was to happen this night...

Kate followed John and Zed out into the hotel parking lot. It was dusk, cold, and cloudy, though the air was clam. Kate turned to John and embraced him tightly. John pushed back slightly and softly cupped Kate's cheek in the palm of his hand. Kate looked up and gazed into John's eyes. The two passionately shared a warm kiss. All doubts and fears seemed to melt away at that moment, as the two slowly pull their soft lips apart.

"I love you," Kate whispered, knowing, without a doubt, how she felt. John looked deep into Kate's eyes. "I know," John said with a smile. Kate could only smile back with a glimmer in her eyes. "Be safe, John Bishop," Kate said as she released her embrace. "You too, Zed! Make sure you got John's back." Kate reached down and toggled Zed's large head between her hands. Zed gave a solid bark and a tail wag to Kate.

"May God protect you in all of His glory, Kate," John proclaimed in his best preacher voice. Kate stood and smiled at John's words. "Have faith, and the rest will follow," John added with a wink.

Kate turned and began to walk toward her car. As she passed John, he quickly reached up and caught her by the wrist as her arm swung from her side. She instantly stopped and looked over her shoulder at John. "I love you," John said, looking into her eyes. "I know," Kate said with a subtle grin. John softly released Kate's wrist and smiled as Kate turned and continued to her car.

Kate opened the door to her Volkswagen Rabbit and clamored into the driver's seat and shut the door. With a turn of the key, the engine started, and she shifted into gear as the car rolled away toward the hospital to be with Preacher.

"Well, bud, are we ready?" John asked. Zed excitedly barked and spun in a tight circle at John's feet. "Alright, let's do this!" John walked as Zed pranced to the nearby jeep. John opened the door, and Zed leaped into the shotgun seat. John got in and pulled the door closed. He turned it over, and the powerful V-8 engine growled as John tuned in the stereo. The speakers began to pump with CCR's "Bad Moon Rising." The jeep's tires squealed on the cold pavement as the vehicle raced down the road toward the church.

The jeep quietly rolled to a stop in the center of the vacant parking lot of the church. John shifted into park and turned off the engine. The door opened, and John and Zed calmly got out of the vehicle. The night was calm, yet cold with a bright moonlight breaking through the scattered clouds illuminating the area in a settle bluish hue.

With his cane in hand, John walked to the front of the jeep as Zed paced by his side. John took a deep, calming breath and reached down, giving Zed a good scratch on the head between his ears. "Ready, bud?" John asked quietly. Zed turned to John with wide eyes and gave a playful low howl with a quick tail wag. John smiled.

Zed suddenly turned and began to sniff the air above. He gave a low growl and took a stance that John knew well. All was quiet... Within a few moments, an unnatural sound began to fill the air. Whispers reached John's ears, sounds of wicked laughter and torment began to echo and break the night silence.

John and Zed looked skyward as the voices intensified. "Here they come," John whispered, patting Zed in the ribs. A figure appeared and floated down to the ground in front of John and Zed. Then another. And another. Now from behind, more shadows began to gather surrounding the two. John glanced around calmly, counting the sets of glowing eyes.

The creatures continued to drop from the skies, while some seemed to appear almost out of thin air. John and Zed stood firm and unfazed as they found themselves thoroughly surrounded by the fiends.

John guessed there to be at least a hundred of the creatures. They stood in a loose circle around John and Zed about 30 feet away in all directions. But John knew, without a command from an Alpha, they would not make a move.

Moments later, there was a parting of a wall of vampires directly in front of where John and Zed were. The fiends moved to either side to clear a path. And there, dressed in a black medieval hooded tunic, stood the Master, Delgado. His evil eyes, glowing under the hood, the monster towered over the rest of his dark army. Almost seven feet tall, a muscular and large frame of a beast, completely healed from his last encounter with John and Zed. And his eyes, glaring with revenge.

"Bishop, the reckoning is upon you," Delgado growled, opening his wide arms and presenting his army. "Well, Merry Christmas to you too, Victor," John replied with a smile and a wave. Delgado could not detect any fear whatsoever from John.

"I have come to collect for what I have asked," Delgado proclaimed, as he methodically lumbered toward John and Zed. His heavy armored leather tunic creaked, and hanging chains of weapons and trinkets clattered as he moved. "The vial, you will give me." Delgado's voice boomed through the air as he spoke. Though as he continued, John's keen hearing picked up on something. John turned his head and honed in on the familiar sound. Delgado continued to talk and threaten as he approached. But John had fearlessly tuned it out. Zed looked up at John and knew by the look on his face, something was causing his anger to build. A flash of a memory struck John. He could see two figures tormenting his wife Amy, in the courtyard. He could hear their laughter as they poked and prodded his beloved. Amy's face covered in splattered blood from the massacre around her. The two vampires, laughing wickedly as they bared their fangs, licked the blood off of her face. "John!" Amy's cries of terror snapped the memory like a brittle stick.

John turned and began to walk steadily toward the two vampires that were joking and laughing. This move caught not only Zed off guard but Delgado as well. John was a few paces out, and Zed had to gallop a few steps to catch up to him. Delgado froze, watching as John approaching the two fiends. As the master vampire stopped in the middle of his threatening rant, his army stood silent as well, as all eyes were on John.

"You the one that killed my Amy?" John asked calmly as he approached the two joking vampires. The vampires stopped laughing. One of the creatures locked eyes with John. "That's right, we killed your unborn child too, ripped him right out of the womb, and we enjoyed it!" The vampire sneered, baring his fangs with an evil grin as he gave a settle glance at his companion, who also chuckle in amusement. John had no clue of the unborn baby until that moment. A look of rage came over his face. One step closer, John was just a few feet away. With one unexpected fluid motion, John pulled his right arm back and threw a hidden trigger in the sleeve of his leather coat. He brought his arm forward, as a   concealed silver dagger launched into his grasp. It was such a quick "sleight of hand" that the creature didn't even have time to react. John slammed the blade upward under the vampire's chin and deep into its skull so hard, the vampire's body left the ground. As it did, the fiend's head exploded into a ball of purple and red flames.

Before the fallen vampire's companion could react, John clicked the boot heel on his right leg. A silver stiletto blade protruded from the boot's toe. As John pulled the dagger from the vanquished creature, he leaped into the air kicking his leg sideways. A look of agony appeared on the vampire's face as John sent a well-placed kick directly into the chest of the shocked monster. Seconds later, the vampire's body reduced to a pile of hot embers.

Delgado wiped the hood from his head, his eyes wide and jaw gaping open from what had just happened. Within but just seconds, he watched John defeat two of his best generals with almost no effort. "Zed, twilight!" John said as he pulled the tip of his cane, flung his wrist, and aimed the shaft at the next closest vampire. A blade sprang from the rod and impaled one of the creatures through the eye socket. A hiss came from the beast as it gritted its fangs and fell to the ground bursting into flames. Again, a burst of fire ignited in the cold air. Zed was already onto another attack of the overwhelmed creatures. The K9 took two of the monsters down within seconds with well-placed bites of his silver fangs, power, and speed.

Chaos ensued, as Delgado's army could feel their Master's fear and confusion. Vampires began to flee in every direction, although some began to advance to stop John and Zed. "Vedo fools, stop otêtez! rip otêtez apart!" (Translated; "You fools, stop them! Rip them apart!") Delgado growled in Vampyric tongue to his minions.

As the Master tried to rally his dark army, John and Zed were still holding their ground against the vampire horde. John stood fearless as he continued to inflict pain and defeat the creatures one at a time. Zed also continued to press walls of the fiends back, as the circle of space around John and Zed began to increase in size. Just as a group of the blood-suckers would rally and rush, John was ready, pulling a crucifix and pushing them back.

After John's radical move, the odds were unexpectedly in his and Zed's favor. But as the night wore on, new strategies came into play. The battle slowed as the vampires regrouped and found a median to work from. John and Zed could hold them back, and take one of the creatures down from time to time, but for how long. Eventually, the numbers game began to work against them.

"I don't know how long we can do this bud. There's just too many of them," John said to Zed, as the two stood back to back. The space between them and the creatures began to get smaller and smaller. John knew the monsters would try and take them in a rush as more and more of the vampires that fled earlier, began to return.

"Your time is up, Bishop!" Delgado growled, towering behind the lines of vampires that were poised to attack. "Give me the vial, we will leave, you will live, and Dyer will be spared," Delgado said as he paced impatiently back and forth behind his army of fanged fiends.

"Lieas all lieas, Victor. Vedo're a coward, êtes hideas behind têm dogas êda leadas têm sheep êon slaughter." (Translated; "Lies all lies, Victor. You're a coward that hides behind his dogs and leads his sheep to slaughter.") John's words brought silence to the vampire herd and rage to Delgado.

The vampire Master stood, glaring at John. "You had your chance, Bishop." Delgado raised both arms to his army. "Us minions, destroy alês town êda consume every soul!" (Translated; "My minions destroy this town and consume every soul!") Delgado growled. The creatures all began to rally to their Master's words. John knew something had to be done quickly before the vampire army started to disperse.

Suddenly, at the end of the road that led into the parking lot, was a set of flashing headlights. "What in the name of," John mumbled as the car sped down the road, honking its unique

German horn. "Oh no," John thought as the Volkswagen Rabbit drove erratically, catching the attention of Delgado and his minions.

John peered through the crowd of vampires and focused on the approaching car. As the vehicle reached the crowded lot, it didn't stop. Thuds and thumps, moans, and groans were heard as the car plowed through the lines of standing vampires. Every few moments, a limp body would go flying through the air, get clipped, or even ran over. Vampires were immortals, although many were, as they were as people, not very smart.

The creatures that got hit or ran over still felt the pain, and within a few moments, they would reset their broken limbs, get up, or just shake off the pain. The car continued to bump its way through the crowd. Soon, the creatures began to move out of its path as not to get hit. As the car took a sharp turn, John was able to see the driver, and it was Kate. "What in God's name," John said softly. All eyes were on Kate and her Volkswagen.

The car veered in a sharp circle. Tires squealing, vampires thumped against the side of the vehicle as bodies rolled to the ground from the impact. The RPMs of the car's small four-cylinder engine topped off as Kate's adrenaline kicked in. John couldn't help to laughed under his breath as he heard Kate attempt a "battle cry" through the half-opened window.

The vehicle made it to a clearing where Delgado stood watching. "No, Kate," John whispered in fear, knowing that the Master vampire could easily and quickly destroy the small car. John saw the brake lights illuminate, and Kate turned the wheel sharp as the tires screeched and the car drifted to a stop yards from Delgado.

Suddenly, the passenger door of the car flew open, and a familiar voice hit John's ears. "Oh my God, no," John mumbled. Preacher Bob clamored out, almost spilling onto the pavement, his crutches clattering to the ground. His entrance onto the battlefield brought a laugh and smile to Delgado.

"You fiend of Hades, you minion of Lucifer, you piece of shit!" Preacher made it to his feet, placing the crutches under his arms to steady himself. Laughter began to spread through the horde of on looking vampires. Delgado himself was enjoying the spectacle laughing uncontrollably as John was nodding his head in disbelief. "Go get him, Preacher," Kate screamed in support from inside the car.

Delgado stood waiting as Preacher clumsily clattered his way toward the vampire. Laughter resonated across the crowded parking lot as John and Zed stood watching from the other side of the crowd.

As Preacher was but a few feet from Delgado, he stopped and took a breath, exhausted from the short trip. Delgado crossed his arms and looked down at Preacher with a smile, waiting to see what Preacher would say or do next.

"Back, spawn of Satan," Preacher bellowed in his sermon voice, producing a wooden cross and pressing it up into Delgado's face with a shaky hand. Almost immediately, Preacher's actions sent Delgado into an uncontrollable evil laugh. Preacher's face fell from the vampire's reaction, and his confidence began to leave him.

Delgado's laughter faded, "Oh really?" he said, shaking his head slightly. The vampire took a step forward as the smile fell from his face. Delgado reached down with no fear and placed his massive open palm onto the cross as Preacher held on tight. Preacher's mouth fell as the vampire squeezed and crushed the crucifix and pulled it gently from Preacher's grasp. "You have to have faith, for this to work on me, Mr. Preacher man," Delgado growled, tossing the kindling over his shoulder. Preacher stood in shock as the vampire stared him down.

Suddenly a cold, powerful claw reached down and clamped around Preacher's neck. He felt himself lifting from the pavement as his crutches dropped clattering to the ground. Inside the car, Kate's eyes widened with fear as John and Zed stood helpless from across the lot. "Wait," Preacher struggled to speak as he lifted further into the air. "I have what you want," he managed to mumble.

Delgado froze. His grip around Preacher's throat softened as he gently placed Preacher to the ground, yet still gripped him by the neck. "And what would that be?" Delgado asked as Preacher balanced himself. He nervously reached into a side pocket of his coat and pulled a crimson glass vial of corked blood. "No, Preacher," John yelled from across the lot. Delgado sneered at John and gave an evil grin.

"Now you said, you would leave and not harm anyone," Preacher said, looking for reassurance. The Master vampire nodded slowly as he gently pulled the vial from Preacher's grasp, still gripping him around the throat.

Delgado slowly pulled the vial closer to examine it. He turned it end to end in his clawed palm, looking for any evidence of tampering. Everything looked right. Preacher began to ease as he could feel the vampire's cold clasp around his neck begin to pull away.

Suddenly, Delgado squeezed Preacher's throat tightly and gazed into his eyes. Preacher began to hear whispers in his head as he fell into a trance. The Master vampire began to search through Preacher's memories. The vampire's mind control was overwhelming as all Preacher could do was to succumb and let Delgado invade his thoughts. Like a book, Delgado flipped the days and nights of Preacher's life, like pages and read each one. The vampire could hear words, conversations, and see what Preacher saw. Meanwhile, John knew what Delgado was doing and could only yell at Preacher, though it was all for nothing.

Delgado's eyes focused as he found what he was looking for from Preacher... A conversation with Kate, brewing a plan to help John against Delgado. The vampire saw Kate helping Preacher in the lab. He saw Kate drawing blood from Preacher's arm. Then she took an empty vial, filled it with the blood, and corked the bottle. She then dipped the corked end into a small puddle of melted red wax. Lastly, Delgado saw images of Kate and Preacher using Delgado's large ring and pressing it into the warm wax to set the "D" into the seal. He then heard the two talk of giving Delgado the vial, hoping it would pass as the original. Delgado would accept it and leave without incident- nearly a perfect plan.

Delgado abruptly broke his mental connection with Preacher and released him from the trance. Preacher shook his head back to reality. He nervously looked the Master vampire in his glaring eyes and smiled. "Hi," Preacher said jokingly, his throat still in Delgado's great clawed palm.

A moment went by, and everything was silent. The vampire gritted his fangs in disgust and tossed the vial as it shattered onto the ground into a small crimson bloodied spatter. Suddenly with great force and speed, Delgado unhinged his jaw and thrust forward, pulling Preacher violently closer. Delgado roared in anger as his fangs dropped ferociously into Preacher's shoulder.

A scream of agony echoed through the air as blood sprayed in all directions, Preacher's eyes widened with terror. "Preacher!" John cried out over the crowd as a blood-curdling scream came from Kate in the car. Cheers and howls of enjoyment resonated from the vampire pack.

Delgado pulled his head back with an evil smile. "I have spared you my fate. You will die, Preacher," Delgado growled. With a mighty toss, Preacher's limp body flew through the air, the sea of vampires parted as Preacher hit the ground and rolled uncontrollably, leaving a trail of fresh blood on the pavement. Seconds later, his body came to rest. Preacher did not move.

Delgado raised his hand to the vampiric horde as Kate fearlessly ran from the car to help Preacher. John and Zed also pressed the vampires to the side to reach their fallen companion. John kneeled and gently put his arm under Preacher and carefully pulled him to a sitting position. Kate covered her mouth and began to cry quietly, seeing the severity of his wounds, knowing there was nothing they could do to save him. Zed stood, holding the line between the vampires and Preacher.

"Brother Bob," John whispered, thumbing blood away from Preacher's eyes. Within seconds, John was covered in blood spewing from Preacher's severed artery. Suddenly, Preacher's eyes fluttered open slightly. "Brother John," he smiled. "It's all ok now. The torment is over," he muttered. "Brother," Preacher's voice became weaker. John pulled him closer as Preacher began to whisper his last words into John's ear.

Within a minute, John marked a cross on Preacher's bloodied forehead with his thumb. He said a short prayer, as Preacher was gone. Kate moved next to John and Zed as Delgado walked the cleared path to confront John and company. As the Master vampire towered over the fallen Preacher, John turned and glared up at the fiend.

John gently laid Preacher's lifeless body to the ground and stood up with Zed and Kate by his side. "And this is how it will end." Delgado's voice boomed as his confidence rose. An evil grin of victory grew on his face. The horde of vampires slowly began to close in on the three. "If only he would have given me what I had demanded, he would still be alive," Delgado said as his minions prepared to attack from all sides.

"And who said he didn't?" John said, fearlessly taking a step toward Delgado. "He lied to me and tried to deceive me. I saw this in his thoughts." The Master sneered as he looked down at John standing before him as vampires flanked, poised to strike.

John calmly smiled... "What is it you say, Victor? Only fools rush in." The grin on Delgado's face fell. "What do you mean, Bishop?" John stood still and calm. "You rushed in, Victor. And you weren't patient enough to listen any further to Preacher's thoughts."

Delgado stepped just a few feet from John, becoming irritated from his games. As he did, he locked his gaze to John and captured him in a powerful trance. But this is what John wanted. Delgado then began to search through John's thoughts.

He came to that night in John's mind. Delgado saw John cradling Preacher and began to hear the whispers of a dying man... "It's all ok now. The torment is over," he muttered. "Brother," Preacher's voice became weaker. John pulled him closer as Preacher began to whisper his last words into John's ear... "We got him, John." A slight smile came over Preacher's bloodied face. "Kate injected me with the vialed blood that he wanted so bad." Preacher giggled in pain from his own words. "Well, he got what he wanted." A look of satisfaction came over Preacher's face.

At that moment, Delgado released John from his trance. A smile grew on John's face as he came to, and saw the anguish on Delgado's face. "Yes, Victor. Preacher gave you exactly what you wanted." John said, staring intently at Delgado. The Master vampire stood still and silent.

Suddenly, Delgado jolted slightly, and his eyes fluttered. A stream of black blood flowed from his left nostril, across his lips and dripped from his long chin. He looked down in shock and felt the blood with a shaky hand. The vampiric virus was already at work in Delgado's bloodstream.

The Master vampire suddenly dropped to one knee as he felt weak and nauseous. The vampire hoard stopped their advance. John now looked eye to eye with Delgado as the vampire became weaker. "It's over, and you're done, Victor," John said with a wicked smile of his own. A rage began to swell within Delgado. He knew John's words were valid, but he would not accept it. "No," the Master vampire growled, mustering his strength out of his anger. He stood to his feet slowly, glaring at John.

"Kill them all!" Delgado roared as his voice rallied the vampire horde into a ferocious and fearless frenzy. The sudden advance of the vampires pressed John, Zed, and Kate into a tight back to back group. They were surrounded. "Oh my God, John, what are we going to do?" Kate squealed as she held a crucifix tight, hysterically trying to fend the creatures back. Zed stood, puffing his fur coat, bearing his silver fangs, awaiting John's command.

As the tension built, John took a breath and seemingly pulled a toothpick out of thin air. Placing the pick between his lips, John glanced over at Kate and gave a wink and a smile. Instantly, Kate's fear began to melt away as she knew, John had something up his sleeve.

John calmly reached into his pocket and found the key fob to his jeep. With the press of a button, the jeep's ignition turned over, and the powerful V-8 engine rumbled through the air. John had a cassette cued up in the stereo, and music began to pump through the powerful speakers. Many of the vampires turned their attention to the jeep, as did Delgado. The song, a familiar one to the Master fiend, Presley's "Can't Help Falling in Love," began to resonate through the cold air. "What is it you say, Victor?" John asked Delgado as the vampire's eyes grew wide. "Oh, yeah. That's it," John said, smiling as he began to sing along to the song. "Wise men say...Only fools rush in." Delgado knew at that moment, it was a trap. But it was too late as John pressed another button on the key fob. A bright, intense light bar mounted on the jeep- front and back, of ultraviolet light, illuminated the surrounding area.

Immediately, Delgado pressed to the pavement hard and cowered under his thick hooded leather tunic. Almost instantly, howls and screams of agony could be heard as vampires began to burn from the intense light. John dropped the tip off of his cane and flung the rod to his side. A silver blade slid from the shaft and locked into place. "Pointy side toward the monsters dear," John said to Kate with a smart-assed grin. "Thanks, babe," Kate replied, snatching the sword from John's grasp with a seductive look. "Zed, twilight!" John commanded as he himself, unleashed a fierce attack upon the creatures.

With two silver daggers in hand and a silver protruding stiletto blade at the toe of his boot, John spun, sliced and stabbed with fluid and calculated strokes. Zed jumped into the air, taking down two of the creatures simultaneously, blue and purple flames blazed all around. Kate turned and stabbed at the agonizing fiends helping to put them to rest.

A few vampires on the outside perimeter of the UV light were able to escape into the darkness though most found themselves burning helplessly as they were hindered helpless.

Another chomp of Zed's silver canines and another burst of flames. Like a game, Zed was having a blast. John continued to cut down one after another as he could feel the tide of battle changing quickly. John glanced over and saw Kate stabbing with confidence, seeming to enjoy the moment. John's plan with the jeep could not have executed any better.

Minutes later, the song played out, John pressed the button on the key fob in his pocket and cut the engine, lights, and music to the jeep. It was quiet. As Kate, John, and Zed stood in the lot, piles of smoldering ash, burnt clothes, and trinkets surrounded them. John meandered around the debris and came to a large mound in the center of the lot.

"Get up," John said, still wielding two readied daggers in hand. The mass began to uncurl, and two dim glowing eyes peered out from under the thick cloth hood. Slowly, the figure rose to its knees in front of John. As it did, Kate and Zed both walked up and stood at either side of John.

"Well played, Bishop," the figure growled. "It's over Victor," John said confidently, as even on his knees, the Master vampire stood nearly as tall as John. With a shaky claw, the vampire slid the hood from his head, his great silver mane, pulling out in clumps with the motion. John could see the vampire's pale complexion was now turning a settle grey with black veins visible just under the creature's cold skin. The virus was spreading through the vampire's body quickly.

Delgado stood alone, on his knees no less. His inhuman strength had left him, and his Vampyric powers had faded. The Master vampire's army was all but defeated. Delgado looked down as a stiff breeze began to stir clouds of ashes from his fallen soldiers all around him, though a wave of anger swelled in his broken body.

John stepped closer. Like a cornered wounded animal, Delgado mustered all of his energy and attempted to bolt away into the darkness. The sudden and unexpected burst caught John slightly off guard. But Zed was ready. A roar of agony pierced through the air as the creature crashed to the pavement. Zed's claws skidded to a stop as his silver canines sunk into the vampire's ankle through his leather boot.

Delgado rolled to his stomach and kicked off his boot and pulled away from Zed in a panic to get away. "Not so fast, Victor." The vampire froze. Two silver daggers crossed his skin at the front of his throat. "All I have to do is pull my arms back, and it's over."

John straddled over Delgado's massive back and held the two blades firmly.

"Do it! Kill me now, Bishop! What are you waiting for! Kill me!" Victor howled, his voice breaking into a settle sob as the torment began to take its toll. The vampire trembled. A tear rolled down his cheek, spitting and grinding his fangs as he prepared to die by John's hand. "No."

John stood, pulling the blades from Victor's throat. John jumped to one side as the vampire rolled to his back. "Killing you would be too easy. I'm going to let you feel what it's like to suffer, Victor." John's words were full of revenge. "You'll die soon enough." John turned his back to Victor showing no fear. "Come on, let's get," John said to Kate, walking away from the vampire.

Delgado watched as John and Kate turned and walked to the jeep. Zed growled at the vampire, still holding the creature's leather book in his jaw like a trophy. Zed calmly walked over to the vampire and spun around slowly. He was almost taunting the vampire. Delgado cowered back, expecting a vicious attack. Suddenly, Zed simply hiked his hind leg and pissed on the Master vampire. With a few last squirts, Zed walked off to join John and Kate at the jeep. As John opened the door, Zed leaped into the vehicle. John reached to the back seat and retrieved a folded blanket.

Delgado sprawled on the pavement in a contorted heap of pain as the virus continued to ravage through his body. He watched as John and Kate solemnly wrapped Preacher's body in the blanket and carefully placed him into the backseat of Kate's car.

Within a few minutes, Kate drove off with Preacher, followed by John and Zed in the jeep, leaving Delgado where he lay. It was quiet, as a large, flaky snow began to fall gently...

The Beginning of the End

Chapter Fifteen

The town of Dyer celebrated Christmas morning solemnly as word of Preacher Bob's death spread. The marquee sign in the churchyard read, "Church Services Suspended Until Further Notice." The groundskeeper closed the panel to the marquee, as the shadow of a jeep slid across the snow-covered lot.

John and Kate exited the vehicle as Zed jumped to the driver's seat. The groundskeeper clamored down the short ladder and limped over to meet with John and Kate. "Merry Christmas," John said, approaching the man with an extended hand. "Merry Christmas to you," the man replied with a groggy voice reaching out to shake John's hand. "You must be Mr. Vincent," John asked, shaking the older man's hand gently. "Yes sir, and you must be John," the man replied with a smile. "I recognize the eye patch," he added. "And Mr. Vincent, this is Kate," John said as Kate smiled at the man. "Merry Christmas, Kate, and please, call me Pete," the man said as he smiled back.

"Well, at least we got a white Christmas! They didn't think it was going to happen," Pete said with a distinct laugh. John laughed and glanced over at Kate, who also giggled at the man's strange laugh. "Well, come with me, and I'll get you situated," Pete said as he turned and limped away. John and Kate followed him up the freshly salted walkway to the church doors.

The door opened, and the three entered. The sunlight sparkled through the numerous windows off the freshly fallen snow. "It's a shame about what happened. He will be greatly missed," Pete said as he stomped his boots just inside the door. "Preacher Bob Klopenstine was a big part of this town's success. And according to him, so are you, John," Pete said, glancing back at John with a smile. Kate looked over at John, smiling and softly rubbed his shoulder.

John and Kate followed Pete down the short hall to Preacher Bob's office. "Let's see here," Pete whispered, flipping on a light switch just inside the door. There was a large antique oak desk set against the wall. It was a work in progress, cluttered with papers, a few small boxes, and holy trinkets.

"Now let's see, I got it here," Pete said as he reached to the pile of papers. He found a thick, sealed manila envelope addressed to the church. "I believe this is it," Pete said as he opened the flap. "Yes, this is it," he said, pulling the short stack of papers from the sleeve and glancing it over.

"I'm sure you will find everything in order," Pete said as he held the envelope of papers to John. "A few weeks ago, Preacher Bob got in touch with his lawyer and set this up. Bob named you, John Bishop, as his successor to this church and congregation in the event of his untimely death." Kate and John looked at each other, slightly shocked at Pete's words. "Congratulations, Preacher John," Pete said with a smile as he patted John on his shoulder. "Here's the keys to the building and his estate." John's and Kate's jaw dropped. "Estate?" Pete laughed his funny laugh. "Why yes! This church is just a small part. He also has a new house on a large piece of property at the edge of town.

"Well, what about his family?" John stumbled over his words, still in shock. Pete took a breath and smiled. "He didn't have any family to speak of. But he had a large extended family of Brothers and Sisters. Pete's crazy laugh once again reared its ugly head.

John solemnly took the keys from Pete's shaky hand. "And here's the address to your new house," Pete said, pulling a folded piece of wrinkled paper from his quilted shirt pocket. "Now, if you'd excuse me, I have to go get ready for the kids. I usually dress up as Santa and pass out the presents at the orphanage." Kate smiled at the thought as John took the piece of paper. "Oh, and by the way, I am the caretaker of this place, so if you have any questions or need anything, my number's on the paper." Pete smiled. "Well, Merry Christmas to you both." Simultaneously John and Kate replied, "Merry Christmas."

Pete turned and walked away toward the door. "Don't forget to lock up now," Pete mumbled, waving over his head as he reached the door. He opened the door and gave a settle cough as the sound of his voice carried through the acoustically designed church. The door closed softly behind the man, and he was gone. John took a deep breath and tossed the keys in his palm and glanced around, "Wow!" Kate smiled and hugged John tightly with excitement. "It's all yours, babe!" John smiled at the notion. "Yeah. When I held Preacher, he whispered to me that the congregation was now mine. But he didn't say so was everything else." John shook his head in disbelief. "Well, let's get," he said as the two snuggled and walked toward the door.

Twenty minutes later...

John turned the jeep onto the long sloping driveway. Freshly salted, it was down to the bare pavement. Elaborately trimmed and equally spaced arborvitaes coated with a light dusting of fresh snow lined each side of the driveway. The drive curved slightly as it opened into a gated courtyard. John pulled up to a three-car garage with elegantly designed doors.

Kate gasped as the attached house looked to be at least three stories. Brick built, with large windows that overlooked acres of land on all sides. A spacious wooden deck set on one side of the large house led to a side patio door and sunroom. A state-of-the-art greenhouse jotted out from the Northeast corner of the foundation, housing many of Preacher's exotic hobby plants. The structure had many characteristic features and designs of the New Dyer Church. John assumed the same architect designed the house for Preacher.

The front door opened as John pulled the key from the lock. Kate and Zed walked into the cathedral-like foyer. The floor was set with intricate marble and slate tiles. Etched randomly with religious symbols, it raised a brow with John.

The house was designed with a very spacious open floor plan. High vaulted ceilings set with aged oak wooden beams, added superior structural strength, not to mention beauty. The house's design was very elaborate for the times.

Suddenly Zed let out a short bark and darted from the foyer down a long hall and around a corner. A moment later, another bark and the sound of ripping paper. John and Kate followed Zed's path as they admired the house and its decor.

Expensive paintings of famous artists, living and past, decorated the multi-colored walls throughout. Antique furniture and unique trinkets created different room ensembles. Thick plush wall-to-wall carpeting in some rooms, weathered stained hardwood floors, and polished marble tiles in others. The house was unique, immaculate, and rich in taste.

John and Kate reached the end of the hall as it opened into a large great room. Kate gasped as a towering decorated fir tree, stood in the center of the room, at least twelve feet tall. It was simple yet magnificently adorned with antique glass ornaments and glittering lights. At the base of the tree, a knitted skirt with golden and white lace. Perfectly wrapped and stacked presents surrounded the tree.

"Zed, what are you doing? Get outta there," John commanded as he suddenly saw Zed's hind end sticking out from under the tree. A moment later, Zed backed out of the pile of presents, wagging his tail. He had a large wrapped package in the form of a giant bone in his jaw.

As John and Kate walked to the tree, Zed sat and began to rip small pieces of the paper from the bone and shake the slivers off his muzzle in a playful manner. Kate covered her mouth in awe as she continued to glance around at the unbelievable house. With a few good rips, Zed had the package unwrapped. It was a giant beef femur bone. John bent down and retrieved a small piece of ripped paper with the name tag. "To, Zed from Bob," John read aloud with a slight smile. Zed wagged his tail, chewing and licking excitedly at the bone. "Ok, bud, ok. Merry Christmas from Preacher," John said with a smile, patting Zed in the ribs.

A faint echo of dainty footsteps from down an adjoining hall caught John's attention. A few moments later, a slim, well-dressed woman, in an apron appeared at the doorway. Her hair was in a tight bun, and although older, the skin on her face was fair and tight, with not a wrinkle. She was carrying a silver platter stacked with decorated Christmas cookies and a small pot of steaming coffee.

"Merry Christmas," the woman said with a warm smile. "Merry Christmas," John and Kate replied, pleasantly surprised. "You must be John and Kate, and of course, Zed," the woman laughed and placed the tray on a side table. "My name is Margret," she said, wiping her hands softly on her apron as she walked toward John and Kate. "Nice to meet you, Margret," John said, reaching out to her for a firm yet delicate handshake. "Nice to meet you," Kate said, also greeting her with a handshake. "I am the head housemaid of the residence," John and Kate turned to each other wide-eyed. "Housemaid," John said, surprised.

"Well, what do you think of your new residence," Margret asked, looking proudly at John. "This is so surreal. I don't know how to take all of this," John said solemnly. Margret smiled and gently squeezed John's shoulder. "Robert was a pleasantly eccentric person who cared for others. And he was very fond of you and Zed. And you gave him a priceless gift." Tears began to build in Margret's eyes, though she smiled at John. "You restored his faith, not only in God, but himself." John dropped his head and sighed.

"But why me?" he asked, shaking his head. Like a Mother, Margret gently placed her hand under John's chin and softly raised his head and looked into his lost eyes. "He saw what you did. He saw what you could do." Kate quietly snuggled to John as she thought the same. "He believed in you, John. Robert saw how you give people hope, and he saw how strong your faith is. And you persevere like no one else he has ever known. And that is why you are the only one he could see leading his parish and congregation." Margret smiled as a heavy tear ran down her face. Kate gently kissed John on the cheek and rubbed his back.

"I'm sure it will take you a few days to let all of this sink in," Margret said with a smile and flourish. "But if you have any questions or need anything, we are always around. And I'm sure you've met my husband, Peter. He is the church caretaker, and he helps with the grounds keeping and maintenance here at the estate. We also have another maid, Ellen Morgan, and a butler, Lynn Belvedere." "Wait, you mean we have a butler named Mr. Belvedere?" John asked. "Why yes, a quite funny English fellow, I think you'll enjoy him," Margret replied. John and Kate looked at each other with a smile, thinking the same thing.

"I have to meet my husband at the orphanage to help with the children. Oh, I almost forgot." Margret turned and walked to the platter of coffee and cookies. She retrieved a white envelope from one side of the tray. "Preacher Bob had this set aside for you," Margret said, walking the envelope over to John with a smile.

John looked down as he graciously took the envelope from Margret's grasp. "Well, I must be off, Merry Christmas to you both," Margret said with a warm smile. "Merry Christmas, Margret," John replied, "To you too," Kate added, clinging to John's side. Margret turned and walked down the hall, around a corner, and disappeared.

"Well, what now?" John mumbled as he looked down at the envelope in his hand. It had his name on it in Preacher's handwriting. "Well, open it," Kate said in excitement as Zed swaggered over with the large bone locked in his drooling jaw. "Ok," John said, flipping the envelope and finding the glued crease. He pulled a small pen knife seemingly from mid-air as Kate shook her head and smiled. "You have to show me how you do that," "Never," John quipped as he slid the razor along the paper's edge. John pulled open the envelope and pulled a folded hand-written letter. As he unfolded the paper, his fingers found a brochure and three glossed cardboard tickets. John took a breath as he began to read Preacher's words...

"Dear, Brother John. Sometimes it is a hard thing to speak the truth without shedding tears. I cannot tell you, or show you, how grateful I am that our paths have crossed. By the glory of God and all that is kind and good, I can only assume this was meant to be. You have done more good in this town than you could ever imagine. And you never asked for anything in return. For me, you have changed my life. For the longest time, I was lost. You and Zed helped me, to not only to find myself, but to also restore my faith and help this small town rise from the ashes of evil into God's greatness. I am proud to call you, not only my friend, but my Brother. You and Zed, together, are the right hand and paw of God.
You deserve a little break, Brother. Please take these tickets and enjoy! One for you, one for Zed (I checked- they do allow service dogs). And one for maybe a special someone. I'm not sure who, but perhaps you can find someone. Merry Christmas! Your Brother, Preacher Bob."

John looked at the face of the tickets. "Oh my God, John," Kate gasped as she also read the cards. "Princess Cruises: The Mexican Riviera. Sun, sand, and stars." John read aloud to Kate. "The Pacific Princess is the essence of elegance, comfort, and unstinting service. Superb cuisine artfully served as only the Italians can. Our British officers, so charming. Our entertainment and musical revues, the finest afloat." Kate covered her mouth in excitement as John continued to read the enclosed brochure.
"No other cruise line visits 5 ports in 7 days. Including Acapulco. Magical places- Cabo San Lucas, Puerto Vallarta, Mazatlan, Manzanillo, and Ixtapa/Zihuatanejo."
"Wow, now all I have to do is find someone to go with me and Zed," John said, placing the tickets back into the envelope. Kate's mouth dropped in shock as John rattled off names.

"Maybe Paula... Or Belinda... Oooo, can't forget Tawny!" John continued to name names as Kate turned red. "John Bishop, how could you!" Kate growled, pushing away from John's side.

As Kate began to storm off, John reached out and caught her by the hand, pulling her firmly into his arms. "Come on, baby," John whispered, "You know you're the girl of my dreams." "You mean it?" Kate asked, looking into John's sultry eyes. "You know I do," John said, leaning in and giving Kate a long, passionate kiss. "Let's go get packed," John said with a grin. "And make sure you pack light!" Kate giggled with delight as the two kissed once again...

That night.

Somewhere, deep, in a city sewer of a vast labyrinth of limestone cut tunnels, an evil was lurking. A large, dark chambered water basin was a sanctuary to a shadowy, ominous figure. Bundled in a heavy leather tunic, his head covered with a large hood sat the battle-worn Delgado.

A dim flood of moonlight cascaded over the vampire's ravaged body from feet above, through a utility hole grate. He sat on a makeshift throne of stone blocks, wooden crates, and rusted, discarded shopping carts. As sewer rats and roaches scurried about, a series of shadows moved silently toward the chamber. Delgado's head turned to the side; his eyes closed as he sat quietly and still. Only his face was visible from under the dark hood. "Esuch downgradae accommodationas prot a Master, sêtetnêo êt no?" (Translated; "Such downgraded accommodations for a Master, is it not?") A deep voice growled. Delgado's dim glowing eyes sprang open. His head slowly turned to the voice.

His vision impaired, Delgado could barely make out the four figures that surrounded him. Though he knew the voice, it was Levi Caspian- the leader of a lesser yet rival Vampire clan. "Ko sêtetnêo êt vedo want, Caspian?" (Translated; "What is it you want, Caspian?") Delgado's voice was labored and rasp. "Êt sêtetnêo time êon step down, Victor." (Translated; "It is time to step down, Victor,") Caspian replied.

There was a moment of silence as the tension grew. "No," Delgado growled and bared his teeth. Only one fang was visible, a void where the other had fallen out. The pack of vampires stood ready as they looked to Caspian.

"Tear otê apart!" (Translated; "Tear him apart!") At Caspian's command, the three vampires viciously engaged in an attack on the ailing Delgado. Indescribable sounds of beasts upon beasts echoed throughout the tunnels. Within a few moments, it was quiet. The three vampires tore the limbs from Delgado's ravaged torso with ease. The Master vampire was able to inflict one of his attackers with only a partial bite, though it was enough.

Spats and pools of black blood were everywhere, on the walls and the floor. Delgado's limbs strewn about as packs of rats rushed in to feast. Caspian walked over to a dark corner. The vampire bent down and picked up Delgado's severed head. He turned the head and looked at Delgado's motionless face. Suddenly, Delgado's eyes shifted and looked at Caspian. Delgado's mouth contorted as his teeth bit into his lips. Blood dripped to the floor as a sudden puff of air spat blood onto Caspian's face, into his eyes, and his mouth. Caspian tasted Delgado's blood as the severed head smiled. In a fit of rage, Caspian squeezed and crushed Delgado's head as if it was a tin can and tossed it to the floor.

Delgado was defeated, although he got the last laugh. The unsuspecting killers had Delgado's blood on their hands and everything else that went with it. The Vampiric virus now had new hosts, Merry Christmas.

A few days later...

The entire town of Dyer shut down on the day of Preacher Bob's funeral. Hundreds of people came from different cities, different states. John and Kate had no idea how respected Preacher Bob was in the religious community, both near and far.

John adjusted his collar nervously, not expecting to deliver a eulogy to this many people. Kate stood by his side, dressed in a conservative black dress. "John, you can do this," she said, rubbing his arm. "I know. But wow, this turnout is amazing," John said, taking a deep breath and glancing at the growing crowd.

Elaborate bouquets of fresh flowers were still arriving and placed on the massive stage, surrounding Preacher Bob's surprisingly simple casket. As people continued to fill the church, John and Kate paced the floor, slowly reading the cards on each flower arrangement.

"Jim and Tammy Baker," John read quietly, looking at Kate. "Jerry Falwell, really?" Kate said, surprised. "Jimmy Swaggart, are you kidding me?" John smiled as the names became more unbelievable. "Billy Gram," Kate read aloud as her jaw dropped.

"No freakin' way!" John said as he stopped in his tracks, reading the next card on the flowers. Kate stepped up to read the card. "John Paul II." John and Kate stood in shock, looking at one another. "He knew the Pope. Preacher Bob knew the Pope." John stuttered, shaking his head as Kate stood wide-eyed. "Oh my God," she whispered. "Pretty damn close," John replied.

In the hour following, John gave a powerful eulogy in honor of Preacher Bob to the standing room only crowd. The sunlight streamed in from the numerous skylights of the building, basking everyone in a Heavenly light. The New Dyer Church choir performed three of Preacher's favorite hymns. Their voices were magnificent, highlighted by the acoustic design of the church's nave. The service was fit for a king, and John knew that Preacher would approve.

As John ended the service to direct everyone out to the cemetery for Preacher's burial, a member of the choir quietly made his way to the stage. "Brother Bishop, please wait a moment." John stopped and turned to face the lead singer of the group.

"Brothers and Sisters of the congregation, friends, family. It is a solemn time." Everyone stopped to listen to the man's words. His thick Jamaican accent was pleasing to the ear. "We have lost a big part of this church. A pillar of strength, and a great leader and confidant of this small town. A brother, a friend." The church was quiet. The only sound was the settle hum of the ceiling fans. "Preacher Bob will be greatly missed from this place. This church was his dream, and he lived to see it fulfilled. And it was also his wish, to have one man continue with what he started. To be our new leader, and to take this congregation into the future." John began to tear up at the man's words.

"I know many of you have not yet met Preacher Bob's successor. So may I introduce him to you at this time." The man turned to John with a smile. "Ladies, gentleman, brothers, sisters. Please join me in welcoming our new preacher, leader, and confidant of this congregation, Brother John Bishop."

Suddenly, the church erupted in thunderous applause. John turned to face the crowd. Faces of smiles and tears stared back at John as a tear rolled down his cheek. John glanced over at Kate, who was in tears clapping and smiling at him in approval. The only fitting thing John could do, he bowed his head gracefully to his congregation.

A sudden bright ray of sunshine came from an overhead skylight and flooded over John. The crowd gasped as John felt a warmth enter into his body. A great clarity and calmness overcame him as he focused on the large gathering before him.

"I thank you. And to fill the shoes of one so admired and beloved is surely an impossible task." John spoke, and his voice was loud and clear. "I have no intention of replacing Preacher Bob. But to carry on his legacy, his teachings, his faith, and his love for this community." John took a step forward toward the capacity audience. "We will not falter Preacher or our God." The crowd was in awe and silent.

"Please, allow us to move Preacher to his final resting place, so his soul may be at peace." At John's words, the crowd silently turned and began to exit the church quietly and in an orderly fashion to the cemetery.

Preacher Bob was laid to rest that solemn day...

Bon Voyage

Chapter Sixteen

Zed laid on his back on the floor. His paws in the air, a chewed leather boot and a beef femur bone on the floor next to him, and a stitched up stuffed doll partially hanging from his open jaw playfully. The T.V. tuned to MTV was thumping to Queen's "Under Pressure," video as Kate and John readied for their cruise.

"Now remember what I said, John." Kate quipped as she unzipped a small carry-on luggage bag. "What?" John replied as he riffled through a duffle bag packing his clothes for the trip. "I said nothing to do with vampires. No garlic, no crosses, no silver daggers," Kate answered as she glanced over at John. "Really, Kate?" John said as his attention, captured by a cut scene of the vampire, Nosferatu in the Queen music video. Kate walked over and clicked off the T.V. "Nothing," she said as she walked back to her packing.

"Well, I'm packed," John said, pulling the zipper. He glanced over at Kate and raised a brow at her small bag. Kate looked at John with a crooked grin. "What?" she asked as she dropped two tiny string bikinis into the bag. "You said pack light," she added with a sexy smile.

A couple of days and flights later.

John, Kate, and Zed entered through the gate to the cruise terminal. It was a beautiful warm and sunny day. Within but just a few hours, the temperature was about sixty degrees warmer from where they came.

John had on his dark shades, Zed had on his leash and service vest, and Kate was giddy with excitement.

As the three waited in the security line, the towering cruise ship floated at the dock. People scrambled about, like ants, boarding, loading, cleaning, and prepping for the voyage.

"Good morning, Madam and Sir. May I please see your boarding documents?" A well-dressed, well-groomed gentleman in sailor attire stood at a small station with a clipboard in hand. "Zed," John quipped as he held onto the harness. The attendant looked down at Zed, who took a step forward and presented the man a muzzle of folded papers. "Ok," the man laughed as he reached down and gently pulled the documents from Zed's jaw.

"Ok, we have your information, and we would like to welcome you to Princess Cruises. We hope you enjoy your voyage with us." The man handed Kate the papers in a small brochure folder with a smile. "Thank you," John and Kate said as they shouldered their carry-ons and walked past the man toward the ship.

About halfway to the ship, the three were greeted by another cruise line staff member also with a clipboard. "Good morning, and welcome to Princess Cruises. May I see your papers please?" the woman asked with a warm smile. Kate handed the woman the papers, and the woman glanced at her clipboard manifest.

"Ok, you are high-status passengers, so please enter the ship at gangway number one, straight ahead. We hope you enjoy your voyage with us." The woman smiled, stamping the documents, and handed two cruise cards and papers back to Kate. "This is going to be so awesome," Kate squealed in excitement as John laughed at her. "I'm sorry, but I have never been on a cruise before," Kate whispered as she tried to collect, herself latching onto John's arm tightly.

John held the harness as Zed towed him and Kate toward the ramp into the ship. Suddenly, a young man wielding a large Canon camera on a strap around his neck approached the three. "Hello and Welcome! My name is David. May I take your picture?" the man asked, leaning back on his foot, uncertain of Zed. John and Kate glanced at one another. "Sure," John said. "Ok, great," David said as he moved to the back of the three. "Let's take one with the ship behind you." John, Zed, and Kate turned, so the ship was to their backs. "Sit Zed," John said as Kate snuggled next to John.

Zed took a seat on the pavement in front of John and Kate. David focused the lens of his camera. "Ok, on three, smile big," David said. "One, two, three, smile!" With that, not only did Kate and John smile, but Zed lifted his lips to expose a smile of teeth and glistening silver fangs. As the man snapped the picture, he pulled back from the camera in shock as Zed's smile caught him off guard.

"The dog smiled at the camera," David said shockingly. "No, really?" John asked, sounding surprised. Kate laughed under her breath as John playfully tormented the photographer. "Sounds like you need a vacation, David," John added with a smile as he patted Zed in the ribs. Kate had to turn from David because she was laughing so hard. "Yeah, I think I do," David mumbled, still in shock. "Your picture will be available onboard at the photo booth," David said, trying to compose himself. "Thank you, David," John said with a smile. Kate was still laughing silently.

Zed rose to his paws, and the three turned and walked toward the entrance ramp to the ship. Another ship attendant stood waiting at the ramp. "Good day to you Madam and Sir." John could not recognize the man's heavy accent. "Welcome to Princess Cruises. May I see your cruise cards, please?" Kate opened the thin folder and found the two laminated cards which had their personal information on them. "Here you are," Kate said as she handed them to the attendant. "Thank you, Madam," the man said with a pleasant smile as he scanned the barcode on each card with a bulky portable scanner. "Thank you, and please enjoy your voyage," the man said as he handed the cards back to Kate. "We will be leaving shortly, so please head to the top deck to say, "bon voyage." Please take the elevator straight ahead to the top deck," the man added.

As John, Zed, and Kate walked aboard the ship toward the elevator, there was steady activity at a cargo door at the ship's stern. Three deckhands were loading a large rectangular crate into the hold. The outside of the box, clearly marked with a red-painted "fragile" on each side of the box.

"What the hell is in the box?" one of the deckhands asked as he helped to push it up onto the ramp. "Don't worry about it," the man's deck officer answered, shaking his head. "The surface of it is cold to the touch," the other deck cadet said as he pushed the cart from behind. "It's from the dry ice," the deck officer replied as he looked at the ship's cargo manifest.

The two deckhands stopped and looked at each other confused. "Dry ice?" One of them asked as they waited for an answer. "Ok, ok," the cargo officer said with a sigh. "I don't want this getting around, and if it does, I know where you don't work anymore, understand?" The two deck cadets nodded nervously in agreement to their superior. "It's a dead body packed in dry ice." The two cadets stood still and quiet for a moment, looking at each other. "What?" one of them blurted out. "Yeah, it's a gentleman who was on vacation and apparently died suddenly. And I guess he's someone important because his family is paying an ungodly amount of money to have his body shipped home."

"Wow," one of the deckhands whispered as the other shook his head in disbelief. "Yeah, so we are quietly shipping him back home. So please keep this to yourself and secure him comfortably in the cargo hold." The officer sternly looked at the two deckhands. "Yes sir," both the men said agreeably.

A sudden voice came over the officer's radio at his hip holster. "Ok, let's hurry up, we just got the five-minute warning. We're shoving off." The officer check marked the cargo on the manifest. "Let's get it secured and get topside for bon voyage." "Yes sir," the two cadets quipped as they pushed the crate into an open bay against the ship's hull.

As the cargo door closed and the ramps retracted from the ship, another deckhand came running into the cargo area. He was holding a large flower arrangement. Somewhat overweight, he was breathing heavily and gasping from the short sprint as the two cadets began to ratchet-strap the crate to the floor.

"Hey guys," the young man said, trying to catch his breath. "Someone said these go with the crate." "Well, we can't open it," one of the deckhands said as he ratcheted the strap tight.

A sudden loud, deep horn resonated through the air. "We have to get topside. Just put the flowers on top of the crate," one of the cadets said as he fixed the cuff on his sailor attire. "Come on! We have to get to our stations." The chubby cadet gave a short nod and tossed the bouquet to the top of the crate. With this, the three raced down the short hall to the freight elevator.

Moments later, the elevator door closed as the elaborate arrangement of fresh flowers immediately began to wilt and die. A sinister laugh came from inside the crate and echoed through the dimly-lit cargo hold. A voice whispered from within... "I'm coming to get you, Bishop. And your little dog too!" A burst of ominous laughter once again filled the air.

Topside on deck, a party was underway. Music was blaring, people were dancing, and confetti was falling from above. The deep bellow of the ship's horn once again reverberated through the warm air as the giant vessel pulled away from the dock. The water around the ship began to churn as the powerful engines turned the massive propeller. A few small tug boats floated along the hull of the ship and helped to maneuver the vessel through the narrow port. A few other tugs followed alongside, sending the cruise ship off with a colorful water salute from fire hoses on board the small, powerful boats.

Kate held John tight and smiled from ear to ear as Zed barked and howled to the excited passengers' cheers. People on the dock followed the ship waiving, whistling, and cheering to the people on board. John smiled, taking in a deep breath of salty air from the tropical breeze.

John leaned in and kissed Kate softly on the cheek. He whispered into her ear, "I love you," as John's voice and warm breath gave Kate goose bumps. She giggled with delight. "We're going to enjoy this," John said as he reached down and toggled Zed's floppy head in his palm. Zed looked at John playfully wagging his tail.

John and Kate turned to the front of the ship, heading into the sparkling crystal blue sea. The two looked at each other and smiled. Their vacation had begun, and it was going to be fantastic. Or so they thought...

The end ¿

Look in the Mirror

Chapter "Unlucky" Thirteen

A warm summer night, the unmistakable sound of two beefed-up Harleys rumbled to a stop outside the crowded roadside bar. Moments later, the front door opened, and two men clad in leather from head to toe walked in as if they owned the place...

"Abe, I told you, but you never listen to me," the first man through the door barked. "John, just drop it, ok?" the second man said, following behind.

"Alright, alright," John said, throwing his hands in the smoky air and turning to Abe. "Can we at least agree on a cold beer?" John asked, shaking his head. "I'll buy the first round," Abe grumbled as the two men turned and walked toward two unoccupied bar stools.

As the two men sat, a scruff of a man came from the end of the bar to greet them. "What can I get ya?" the man mumbled. "Two beers," Abe said, gesturing with "rabbit ear" fingers. "Tap's down, bottles ok?" the man muttered. "As long as they're cold," Abe replied. The barkeep reached down into a nearby cooler and pulled two bottles of cheap beer, popping the cap on each one before placing them in front of the two patrons.

"Ahhhh, ice-cold piss water," John said with a smile taking a quick swig of the bitter beer. Abe joined in on a sip of his bottle with a slight cringe. "Well, at least it's cold," Abe commented, shaking his head from the bitter taste.

The two men swiveled their stools around and scanned the smoke-filled pub. About thirty people were mingling about. A waitress was at a corner table, getting a fanny slap from a man as she placed another beer on his table. A few huddled at a table playing a drunken game of cards. Others were mingling about telling bad jokes or merely trying to pick up someone to get laid.

Abe's attention turned to a pool game as a cue ball cracked into a new rack of balls. The table was surrounded by a group of roughneck bikers who looked worse for wear. John and Abe could see a crooked stack of wrinkled money on the corner of the table, waiting for a winner.

John and Abe glanced at each other with a grin. "Well?" Abe looked at John. "Go for it," John said, egging him on. "Yeah, why not," Abe whispered, leaning forward off the stool with a beer in hand. "Hey," John quipped, pulling a twenty from his jacket pocket. "Half the pot is mine." Abe smiled, taking the bill from John between his fingers. "Just make sure you got my back," Abe said, glancing up at the pool table of thugs. "Looks like I'm walking into a Goddamn viper pit." John laughed at his words. "Sure, I'm ready if you are!" "Be back in a minute," Abe said, taking a breath as he walked away toward the table through the smoke.

As Abe reached the group at the table, John's attention turned to a sultry waitress passing by. "Hi there, sugar," she said in a sexy voice, her blue eyes locking with John's. He smiled and gave a settled wink. "Hey there." The waitress stopped in front of John. "Can I get you anything, anything at all?" she asked, reaching over and twirling a length of hair on John's shoulder. John grinned as she pulled in closer, separating his legs with hers. "I think I'm good for now, but maybe later," John whispered as he also leaned in close, letting his palms fall and rest on her hips. "Ok, sugar. Just let me know. By the way, my name's Candy," the waitress said with a seductive look as she leaned in closer. "I get off at eleven." John got goose bumps as she whispered in his ear. John grinned, as the waitress reluctantly pulled back and continued on her way to wait on other customers. John took another sip as he glanced over to the pool table. With cue stick in hand, Abe was able to sneak in and start a game of eight ball with the winner of the previous game.

With a solid stroke of the stick, the cue ball smacked the fresh rack of balls. Abe had on his best poker face as he moved around the table for his next shot. The time went quick, as Abe cleaned the table easily. Double or nothing, the tension grew halfway through the second game. Then into the third game, the pile of money grew.

Tempers grew short as Abe finished the third game, pulling the wad of cash off the table and into his jacket pocket. "Gentleman," Abe said as he carefully walked away, ready to be attacked from behind. John sat prepared to spring from the stool at the first sign of trouble.

John peered around Abe, making sure he was safe as Abe took a stool next to him. "You feel that?" Abe whispered as he separated the wad of cash from his pocket. "Yep," John said, swiveling the stool back to the bar. "Here's your half," Abe said, giving John his half of the money. "Damn, that was easy," John remarked. "Yeah, way too easy," Abe added as he motioned to the barkeep for another beer.

"You know they're going to try something," Abe said. John nodded in agreement. "Yep!" "Well, we got one thing going for us. Half of them are drunk." Abe said, glancing over his shoulder. "And only half of us are drunk too," John said with a buzzed smile.

Abe took a sip from his bottle. He took a hard gulp and froze. "John." The tone in Abe's voice suddenly changed. "What?" John asked, checking over his shoulder with glassy eyes. "Look in the mirror behind the bar," Abe said quietly. John looked up and into the mirror that ran the length of the bar. "Oh, my God! Either that mirror is extremely dirty, or you are one ugly son-of-a-bitch!" John said jokingly, looking at Abe. "Nope! You're just one ugly son-of-a-bitch!" John began to laugh at his own words. "No, John, look in the mirror, behind us," Abe said quietly yet sternly. John took a breath and bobbled his head back to the mirror.

John took a swig on his bottle and swallowed. Slowly, he began to realize what Abe realized. John focused on the mirror. There he was, as was Abe... But behind them, there was no one. John slowly turned and looked behind him. The pub was full of people. John once again turned to the mirror and saw only him and Abe. "Shit," John mumbled. "Yeah, we're deep in it," Abe said nervously. "You're on the clock Bishop," Abe said in a serious tone. "I need you to sober up now!" "Right," John growled, mustering himself to a straight head.

"You packing?" John asked as he pushed the half-empty bottle away from him. "Nope. I've got a blade in my belt, and one in my boot," Abe said quietly as the patrons began to take up strategic positions in the bar. "What have you got?" Abe asked as the tension grew. "Nothing any better. A crucifix necklace and a knife in my pocket." John whispered, shaking his head. "Damn, we're gonna have a hellofa time getting outta here alive," Abe said, glancing around. "Ya think so," John quipped.

"Ok, smartass keep a straight head. The big guy at the door just locked us in." Abe said as he carefully reached to his belt to ready his blade. John calmly spun around on his stool to face the crowd catching Abe off guard. As John scanned the room, all glowing eyes were on him and Abe.

John turned and focused on a familiar face in the crowd. "Hey sugar," Candy said, walking by with glowing yellow eyes and a smile, flashing her fangs. She took a stand at a table, behind a line of growling vampires.

"John, what the fuck are you doing?" Abe asked under his breath as his grip tightened around the hilt of his blade. John turned nonchalantly toward Abe. "I don't quite know. I'm making this shit up as I go. Just be ready." John hopped off the stool to his feet. He was loaded with liquid courage and showed no fear as the hoard of vampires prepared to attack.

John turned toward the nearby wall where a short, portly man with greasy straggly hair stood in front of the jukebox. He stared with glowing eyes and glistening fangs as John approached. The vampire hissed as John stopped in front of him. John brought his index finger up to the creature, signifying to hold on a moment. John reached over to a nearby table. There were a few discarded drinks left from the previous occupants.

John picked up a half-full glass of strong alcohol. As he guzzled the liquid, John still had his finger up to the waiting vampire. But John also had a little surprise clenched in the palm of his hand. John carefully placed the emptied glass down to the table, diverting the creature's attention.

John dropped his finger and maneuvered a small lighter in his palm. John rolled his thumb on the flint wheel, and a low flame ignited. The vampire looked down at the small dancing flame that John held to his twisted face and began to laugh. John smiled at the creature. All the other vampires watched and waited in bewilderment at John's unorthodox action, as did Abe. John had an audience, and the show was about to begin...

Suddenly, John leaned forward and, with a hefty blow of air, spit a full mouth of flammable liquid at the lighter's small dancing flame. An intense fireball launched at the vampire's face as the creature screeched in terror. The fiend's face and hair exploded into an inferno as the monster flailed about uncontrollably from the intense pain. John quickly flipped a nearby chair to his grasp with the end of his foot. With a rush of adrenaline, John swung the chair at the blinded vampire. With a mighty blow, the chair smashed to pieces into the flaming maniac. The vampire, out on his feet, fell back into the idle jukebox, jolting it from its place and then fell to the floor in a burning mass. Suddenly the jukebox came to life from the impact. The machine shuffled a moment through its collection then dropped a record onto the turntable.

"Abe, now," John yelled, as Blondie's "One Way Or Another" began to pump through the box's speakers. The room of vampires stirred, and their attack was underway. "Shit," Abe mumbled as one of the creatures was there instantly. Abe stood from the stool just as the beast came with a powerful backhand that sent him tumbling backward over the bar.

As Abe clattered to the floor, he sat up just as the vampire jumped to the top of the bar. The monster opened his arms and growled, bearing its fangs, glaring at Abe as he got ready to pounce. Something suddenly caught Abe's attention. He looked to a shelf directly in front of him, and there, a sawed-off shotgun. Quickly Abe bucked at the shelf, and the board bounced the weapon off and down onto his shin. Abe pulled his leg back and kicked the gun into his grasp. Abe raised the double-barrel with not a second to spare and pulled the trigger as the vampire dropped down to meet him.

The blast from the powerful gun sent the attacking beast flying backward, tumbling through the air in a heap. "There's more shells in that box by the tap." A nearby voice caught Abe off-guard. He turned, and there was the barkeeper, also hiding behind the bar. "They're loaded with rock salt and silver oxide. It's my own recipe," the man said with a smile. Abe nodded as he collected a few shells from the box and reloaded. "Sometimes, I need to use it. Even drunk vampires can get out of control once in a while." The man smiled and shrugged his shoulders. "You got any more guns?" Abe asked, peering over the top of the bar to check on John. "No," the man replied, shaking his head. "But I've got this." The man reached behind a keg and produced a wooden bat, set with sharp silver studs. "Can I borrow that?" Abe asked with a grin. "Sure," the man said, holding the handle to Abe. With a smile, Abe took the handle of the bat and rose to his feet from behind the bar.

"Hey, John," Abe yelled out over the music. John turned as he was fending off a vampire with a chair. "Swing for the fence," Abe said as he tossed the bat over the bar to John.

With a twist of the chair, John was able to tangle up one of the attacking creatures long enough to catch the handle of the bat in his grasp. As the vampire broke free to continue its attack, John met it with a vicious swing of the bat to its head. The wooden bat with the silver embedded studs did the job exceptionally well. The vampire's skull caved, as teeth exploded from its jaw. The creature's head loafed about as its body collapsed to the floor in a burning heap.

Two more vampires moved in to face John. "John down," Abe yelled as he was now standing on top of the bar. John dropped as Abe pulled the trigger. One of the monsters flew off its feet from the powerful blast, flying backward violently over a table and to the floor. Before the other creature could react, John was to his feet with a swing of the bat. Another well-placed headshot immediately took down the vampire.

Vampires scattered about, growling and hissing in anger. They tried to flank John, but Abe was there as a cut-off point. Abe was able to take three of the creatures out of the equation with two pumps and trigger pulls of the sawed-off shotgun. John continued to fend off advancing monsters with well-placed swings of the silver-studded bat.

"There's just too many of them," John said as he side-stepped a half-drunken fiend and backed up to the bar. "Yeah, but half of them are not sure about attacking us. We're pushing them back," Abe remarked as he quickly reloaded two shells from his jacket pocket. "Yeah, but for how long?" John said as he cracked another vampire in the skull.

John's adrenaline was working for him as his head was clearing quickly. And Abe knew, with a "clear-headed" John, they had a chance. "Abe, what's that? There's one in each corner," John pointed the end of the bloodied bat at an odd reflective object set in a light fixture. "See it?" John asked as he brought the bat back and readied another swing. "I see it," Abe answered as he jumped back behind the bar.

The barkeep still huddled behind the bar in a corner, heard John's question. "I know what he's talking about!" The man got excited as Abe looked down at him for an answer. "So," Abe said. "What is it?" "They're black lights," the man answered, peering cautiously over the bar. "Years ago, we use to have black light parties to promote new records." The man dived to the floor as another vampire tried to attack Abe. Another blast from the shotgun sent the fiend flying backward through the smoky air. "And black lights are UV. Good eye, John," Abe mumbled with a grin on his face. "John, they're black lights," Abe yelled across the bar. "Can you please find the switch," John screamed back as he parried an attack from the side. "Where's the switch for the lights?" Abe asked the cowering man. "There's a switch in the corner, along the back wall. I don't even know if they work anymore. They haven't been turned on for years." The man once again dove out of sight.

"Well, let's just hope. John, back wall in the corner," Abe yelled. John turned and saw the jumbo commercial switch. But there were about ten to twelve vampires between him and the switch. "John, it's now or never. They're going to rush us," Abe bellowed as he turned to the hoard of vampires charging to attack from the opposite side of the room.

With only two shells left in the barrels, Abe jumped down and stood between John and the attacking creatures. "Shit," John growled as he rushed the group of vampires fearlessly swinging wildly with the bat. He focused on the light switch and was determined to reach it. It was their only chance.

Abe took aim and pulled the trigger. Both shells fired and hit three and grazed two more of the attacking monsters. But there were too many. Abe hit one with the butt of the gun before being tackled onto a table then crashing to the floor. John pushed forward, taking down three of the fiends before his attack was smothered.

One after another, John could feel powerful grasps impeding his movement. He leaned forward, with one hand still free and holding the bat tightly. John felt himself being pulled down to the floor. With one last burst, John pulled back his arm and launched the bat free from his grasp.

The bat spun in the air as John hit the floor hard. Abe grappled in a heap on the floor nearby, stabbing wildly with his silver knife. As if in slow motion, John and Abe focused on the airborne bat spinning toward the light switch.

A moment later, the bat "tinked" against the wall and missed its mark clattering to the ground. John and Abe both moaned in disappointment as the bat rolled to a stop on the floor. With the fight coming to an end, so did the song on the jukebox.

With John and Abe helplessly pinned to the floor, the remaining vampires regrouped and circled around the two. A towering figure came through the haze from behind. Abe recognized him as the vampire who locked the door before the attack, more than likely the group leader. "Êtez will inflict pain upon otêtez, then êtez will feast upon otêtez." (Translated; "We will inflict pain upon them, then we will feast upon them.") A wave of sneers, growls, and laughter spread through the hoard. "Get otêtez êon têmez feet," (Translated; "Get them to their feet,") the alpha said as he took a step back. With this, the two men were lifted to their feet and held securely in place.

The alpha vampire lumbered a few steps to where John was held immobile by four other vampires. John looked at the creature with anger in his eyes. The vampire grinned at John's misfortune baring his fangs. "So, kê'as vút master, bitch boy?" (Translated; "So, who's your master, bitch boy?") John mumbled, trying to keep his temper in check. The vampire's grinning face fell. Mumbles and gasps came from the vampires as John's knowledge of their tongue caught them off guard. Abe calmly kept quiet as he was also held in place.

The alpha leaned in, inches from John's face as his glowing eyes darted all over John's face, and his lip began to twitch from anger. "I have no master, bitch," the vampire growled. Fearlessly, John raised his head and locked gazes with the creature. "I know a master when I see one. You're no master." John whispered as he could feel the vampire's anger growing. "You're bat shit!" John added, keeping his gaze locked and not a blink.

Abe closed his eyes and shook his head, knowing John had pushed too far. Suddenly, the vampire's eyes widened, and its jaw unhinged. With great force, the vampire roared in anger. John could smell death from its putrid breath as the creature's long tongue whipped around, and its fangs protruded less than an inch from John's face. John's hair blew as he stared into the vampire's gaping mouth.

The creature's mighty roar subsided as the vampire pulled back slightly. "Looks like you have a cavity. You might want to get that checked." John said with a smile. Abe dropped his shaking head and laughed under his breath at John's stupidity and or bravery.

The vampire's rage grew even more as John was unphased. Suddenly the alpha looked up behind John and saw the barkeeper trying to creep unnoticed along the wall. All eyes were now on the man who made his way over to the back corner.

The man stopped and turned to face the quiet crowd. "Oh, hi," he said with a nervous wave and smile. All the vampires stood silent, unaware of the man's intent. The man turned, took a step, reached up, and flipped the switch.

Only a few of the ultraviolet bulbs illuminated, a couple popped from age, but it was enough. After a few seconds, screams and howls of pain filled the bar. A smell of rotting burning flesh filled the air as the vampires began to scatter in terror, as their skin and hair burned and singed from the UV light. John and Abe were suddenly free as the creatures scurried for cover.

The alpha stood watching the skin on his massive arms, and hands begin to blister and burn as he growled in anger. John, now free, quickly pulled his silver blade from his pocket. Without a second to spare, John thrust the knife under the vampire's chin into his skull. The massive vampire dropped to his knees as his head burst into a crimson and purple ball of fire. A moment later, the vampire's lifeless torso fell to the floor in a pile of ash and embers. John straddled the smoldering corpse and reached for a set of keys to the front door.

Abe kicked and flipped tables, as the creatures tried to hide from the light. John did the same as they corralled the vampires to the corner of the bar where the UV light rays couldn't reach. The creatures were trapped. "Well, the odds are back in our favor," John said, pulling a smoke from his jacket pocket and tossing the pack to Abe. "Barkeep, how about a drink?" John said as the barkeeper smiled and ran behind the bar to fetch a couple of cold beers. "Just one, John," Abe remarked as he lit his smoke. John nodded with a grin.

John and Abe meandered through the flipped tables and chairs and met at the bar. "Here's two cold bottles of my best, on the house, of course." The bartender flipped the caps off and slid the bottles within reach.

"So, what's your name, barkeep?" Abe asked, taking a puff on his cigarette, reaching for a bottle. "Lloyd." The man said, wiping his palm on his bar apron. "Well, Lloyd, thanks for the help," John said as Lloyd smiled. "So, what's your story?" John asked, sipping on his cold beer. "Well, my brother and I opened this bar years ago. And last year, one night, these bikers stopped in for a drink and a game of pool. Then every night afterward, they would come back with more of their friends. And slowly, all of our regulars began to disappear, one by one." John and Abe listened contently to the man's story as they sipped on their beers. "Then, one night, my brother and I decided to take a stand and run them out of here." Lloyd shivered slightly as the vampires hissed and growled in the corner like trapped animals. "Well, I take it didn't go very well," John said, glancing back at the monsters who were frantically trying to figure a way out. "No," Lloyd said, shaking his head. "They made it known to us that night, what they were, and threatened us. My brother, Clarence, tried to fight them, and they killed him." Lloyd was on the verge of breaking down as he continued. "So, they threatened me, and told me they would let me live if I served them. So that's what I do." Lloyd's eyes filled with tears.
"That's what you did," Abe said sternly. "That ends tonight," he added. Lloyd smiled at the notion. "Well, let's end this, shall we," John said with a smile, finishing off the bottle. "You can wait here if you want, John and I can handle this," Abe said as John walked over to the back corner of the building. "No, I want to help," Lloyd said, standing straight. "I need to do this," he added, taking in a deep breath. Abe smiled, "Ok, then."
John reached to the floor and retrieved the silver-studded bat and gave it a solid grip. Abe walked over, picking up a pool cue, and looked at the group of corralled vampires. They wanted to attack, but the UV light kept them at bay. John made his way back to the bar and stopped at the silent jukebox.

Abe returned to the bar and cracked the pool cue across the edge of the counter. It splintered into two pieces. He handed one to Lloyd. "Your weapon, sir," Abe said with a grin. Lloyd smiled and reached for the cue. "You know how to use that?" Abe asked. Lloyd shook the splintered stick. "Stake through the heart," Lloyd said with an angry look toward the monsters. "Stake through the heart," Abe said, smiling tapping the end of his stick to Lloyds. "We'll let John take them down first, then we'll do our thing," Abe added. "Hey, John, ready to finish it?"

"Yep," John said, twirling the weight of the balanced bat in his grasp. "But first, how about some vampire killing music." John approached the jukebox and pulled a quarter. "Let's see here," John mumbled, scanning the catalog of tunes. "Ah, perfect!" John placed the quarter in the coin slot and pressed "E4". John turned and proceeded toward the hoard of vampires in the corner with Abe and Lloyd following behind on each side.

John stepped to the edge of the circle of vampires, as the juke-box dropped a record. A/C D/C's "If You Want Blood (You Got It)" began to pump through the speakers and set the tone. The vampires cowered, feeling helpless and trapped, hissing, and growling as John showed no fear. "Hey, there sugar." John turned his head, and there was Candy. Her eyes glowing faintly, burn scars on her cheek and forehead. She smiled, baring her fangs, licking her ruby lips. "What can I do for you?" she asked with a sexy voice. "I'll do anything you want," she said, attempting to use her vampiric powers to seduce and hypnotize John with her gaze. But she was weak, and he was strong.

John smiled as Candy nervously smiled back. "Sorry, babe. I like my Candy, sugar-free." John pulled back, choked up on the bat, and got ready to swing for the fence. Candy hissed, her face falling into a hideous frown of anger as the slaughter began...

About The Author

Cory C. Kovacs

Cory Kovacs was a product of the '70s. Born in 1971, he grew up in the times of creative toys, great music, and a plethora of endless cartoons. With the animated empires of Hanna-Barbera, Looney Tunes, and Tom and Jerry to grow up on- the stage was set.

Cory had a passion for humor and with the Star Wars films, an eye for science fiction. The '70s and '80s also led into a time of great "slasher" and horror movies, including such films as "The Texas Chainsaw Massacre," "Halloween," "Friday the 13th," to name a few. This fueled a liking for the horror genre for Cory.

In 1979, the release of a mini-series based on a book from a new author named Stephen King greatly influenced Cory. To this day, Salem's Lot is one of Cory's favorites and still gives him chills. Along with 1985's Fright Night, Cory's love for vampires was born.

Fresh out of high school, Cory pursued a dream career of stand-up comedy and had moderate success in being a featured act and house MC at well-known Comedy clubs in the Midwest and Southeast comedy circuits. This is where Cory honed his skills in humor and writing his own material.

Then, in about 1992, Cory purchased a Smith Corona typewriter and began to peck out the beginning of "Mortal Dire." As life stepped in, his writings got pushed to the back burner. The typed pages in a manila envelope, in a folder, in a chest, in a basement.

Fast forward into his 40's, with a computer, the internet, the ability to "self-publish," and a glance at Cory's bucket list, a book or two needed to be written.

Also, being an avid animal and dog lover, Zed was born and cast as one of the main characters in the story. Zed's character is based on Cory's beloved dog, Ernie, who past a few years back.

Growing up in the '80s, a love of horror and vampires, a love of dogs, with a twist of humor- The recipe to Mortal Dire.

Books In This Series

Mortal Dire

Book One, Barlos

Vampire hunter and ordained minister, John Bishop, is teamed with an unlikely partner in Zed, a German Shepherd with silver fangs. Set in the glorious '80s, in the small rural town of Dyer, John and Zed must hunt down and destroy an alpha vampire who has taken over the community. Along the way, faced with incredible odds, a veil of mystery is lifted, to reveal more questions than answers. Get ready for classic horror, nostalgia, humor, and twists and turns at every page!

Book Two, Delgado

John Bishop and his faithful K9 companion, Zed, return to Dyer after receiving an intriguing phone message. During the demolition of the old Dyer church, a small locked chest is discovered. Knowing Zed had found the possible key, Preacher Bob does his best to get the message to John. However, someone else finds this out as well. A sinister evil once again invades the small town of Dyer to claim what is in the locked chest. John and Zed must face off against the dark fiend and discover the chest's mysterious contents before it's too late.

Books By This Author

Mortal Dire, Book One, Barlos

The first book in the Mortal Dire series.

Made in the USA
Monee, IL
21 September 2020

43146040R00100